STARTING
from
SENECA
FALLS

ALSO BY KAREN SCHWABACH

The Hope Chest

A Pickpocket's Tale

The Storm Before Atlanta

STARTING *from* SENECA FALLS

KAREN SCHWABACH

RANDOM HOUSE 🏠 New York

Text copyright © 2020 by Karen Schwabach
Jacket art copyright © 2020 by Kelly Anne Dalton

Photograph credits: Elizabeth Cady Stanton Papers/Library of Congress (p. 217); Frank W. Legg Photographic Collection of Portraits of Nineteenth-Century Notables/National Archives (p. 218); © Illustrated London News Ltd/Mary Evans (p. 225); New York Public Library (p. 228); Pendleton's Lithography/Library of Congress Prints and Photographs Division (p. 226); Samuel J. Miller/Wikimedia Commons (p. 216).

Visit us on the Web! rhcbooks.com

Educators and librarians, for a variety of teaching tools, visit us at
RHTeachersLibrarians.com

Library of Congress Cataloging-in-Publication Data
Names: Schwabach, Karen, author.
Title: Starting from Seneca Falls / Karen Schwabach.
Description: New York: Random House Children's Books, [2020]
Summary: In 1848, eleven-year-old Bridie runs away to Seneca Falls, New York, where she meets a free black girl named Rose and gets caught up in Elizabeth Cady Stanton's plans for a women's rights convention. Includes historical notes.
Identifiers: LCCN 2019037551 (print) | LCCN 2019037552 (ebook) |
ISBN 978-0-593-12505-2 (hardcover) | ISBN 978-0-593-12506-9 (lib. bdg.) |
ISBN 978-0-593-12508-3 (ebook)
Subjects: LCSH: Woman's Rights Convention (1848 : Seneca Falls, N.Y.)—Juvenile fiction. | Stanton, Elizabeth Cady, 1815–1902—Fiction. | CYAC: Woman's Rights Convention (1848 : Seneca Falls, N.Y.)—Fiction. | Stanton, Elizabeth Cady, 1815–1902—Juvenile Fiction. | African Americans—Fiction. | Seneca Falls (N.Y.)—History—19th century—Fiction.
Classification: LCC PZ7.S3988 St 2020 (print) | LCC PZ7.S3988 (ebook) |
DDC [Fic]—dc23

Printed in the United States of America
10 9 8 7 6 5 4 3 2 1
First Edition

Random House Children's Books
supports the First Amendment and celebrates the right to read.

TO SUKY & JAMIE
AND TO
ELIZABETH NIELDS
WITH LOVE
(AND ELEPHANTS)

CONTENTS

1

TAKEN ON TRIAL

The cell was five feet by nine feet and stifling hot. It contained a bucket, a pile of dirty straw, and Bridie. And it smelled of the bucket.

Up near the ceiling was a small, barred window. Bridie jumped up, managed to grab the bars, and walked herself up the wall. She had to turn her head sideways to peer out.

Through the small slit she could see the fields and the woods. And just a corner of the graveyard . . . she looked away quickly. She could see the other poorhouse children out in the cabbage field, weeding. A couple of the best-trusted boys were using hoes, but the rest of the children were down on their knees, pulling up weeds with work-roughened hands.

The children were nearly all younger than Bridie, who was eleven. Boys and girls her age were usually indentured soon after they came in. Especially if they came in with their parents. Parents who had ended up in the poorhouse were not considered suitable company for their own children.

But Bridie had been allowed to stay while her mother's illness lasted. And now that that was over with . . . well, Bridie was trouble.

She asked questions. She pointed out the problems with things. She had opinions about the way things ought to be. She spoke when not spoken to.

And so here she was, locked up again on bread and water.

Beyond the fields she could see the woods, where the boys and men cut wood for the fires and for the poorhouse keeper, Mr. Fitch, to sell.

The poorhouse was out in the middle of nowhere, far from the bustling towns of the Finger Lakes. Because the poorhouse housed the people nobody wanted to have to see. Not just poor people, but folks who had turned out simpleminded, or been injured badly at work, or had just gotten too old to work, or had become a bit peculiar.

Bridie heard iron-tired wheels out on the road, and the clop of a horse's hooves. She cricked her head around, trying to see if it was a buggy or a wagon. Then the sound of its wheels was drowned out by howling.

Old Mad Janet had gone off again.

Ha. They'd be sorry now that they'd locked Bridie up. She was just about the only person who could manage Mad Janet.

Then Bridie had another thought. There were only four cells in the poorhouse—only two for women and girls. If they locked Mad Janet up, they might have to let Bridie out.

They weren't supposed to keep you in the cell on bread and water for more than two days; that was in the rules. But they did. Bridie thought she had been here for longer, boiling all day and freezing in the cold upstate New York summer nights. She had kept time by the gong that awakened the inmates at dawn, and the gongs that called them to their silent meals, and the gong that called them to Sunday prayers, and the gong that sent them to bed.

At least three days. Maybe four.

"Rubbish bums!" yelled Mad Janet. "Take the mouse war! They were old and fine and my people were kings, you know, kings! While yours were slippery dockets and all the whales!"

Bridie let go of the bars and dropped, her feet hitting the wooden floor with a thump.

Mad Janet kept going. "KIIIIINNNNGGGGSSS!"

CRASH! Something hit the wall—maybe a wooden bench. If Janet was throwing things, that could be Bridie's ticket out of here.

There was the sound of a scuffle. Mad Janet yelled and cursed. Bridie braced herself to run out the second the door opened—if it did.

Mad Janet let out a low-pitched, keening howl. It came closer as they dragged her up the stairs.

Now, which cell would they open?

Bridie held her breath and hoped.

The door swung open. Mr. Fitch and his son wrestled Mad Janet into the room.

Mad Janet looked at Bridie for a moment with perfect clarity. "I splotted the turnkeys, matey," she said. "It's bows and anchors to yours, and mink jelly on Thursdays."

"Thank you," Bridie whispered, and darted out. She ran across the women's ward and down the stairs, eager to be outside at last in the clean air.

But Mrs. Fitch stood at the bottom of the stairs, blocking her way. "Where do you think you're going?"

"Out to the cabbage field to work," said Bridie. "Mr. Fitch told me—"

"No, he didn't. In here." She grabbed Bridie by the collar and marched her into the office.

It was a bare room, like all the others. The whole place smelled of failure and boiled cabbage. Painted on the wall in tall black letters were the words WORTHY OF NOTICE: SELF-GOVERNMENT, QUIETUDE, AND PEACE ARE BLESSINGS. There was a table, two chairs, and a stack of ledgers, recording each poorhouse inmate's date of arrival, personal information, and (in parentheses, where applicable) date of death. Bridie's name was in those ledgers, she knew.

So was her mother's.

A large man was sitting in one of the chairs. He looked like he could lift a full-grown hog under each arm, and throw both hogs at you if he didn't like you. He stared at Bridie as if he didn't like her.

"Scrawny little thing, ain't she?" he said.

Bridie didn't like *him* much either. But she held her tongue; she'd only just gotten out of the cell.

A tall, thin woman with a face like a missed dinner stood beside him. "Any help I can get, Mr. Kigley—"

"Did I ask you to speak?" said Mr. Kigley.

Mrs. Fitch seated herself at the table and opened a ledger. "These are the Kigleys," she told Bridie.

Bridie stood there and looked at Mrs. Kigley. Mrs. Kigley looked back, her mouth a thin hard line.

5

Then Bridie glanced down at the open ledger. She saw her own name.

Brigid Gallagher. Born: Ireland. Aged 11 yrs. Admitted with mother (mother died May 9, 1848).

Mr. Kigley was still looking Bridie over. "How much?" he asked.

"It costs nothing to take a poorhouse child on trial," said Mrs. Fitch.

"I mean, how much will *you* pay *me*?"

"We do not," said Mrs. Fitch. "You will have the girl's labor, and that is payment enough."

Mr. Kigley didn't seem to like that. "What if I get her bound over? Might as well buy the whole hog."

"We prefer that you take them on trial," said Mrs. Fitch firmly. "To ensure that all parties are satisfied with the arrangement."

Mrs. Fitch and Mr. Kigley gazed at each other, hard and intractable.

"Let me talk to your husband," said Mr. Kigley.

The stairs creaked as Mr. Fitch and his son descended. Mad Janet's low keening was a distant howl in the background, like dogs in the night.

Mr. Kigley heaved himself to his feet, and he and

Mr. Fitch shook hands and talked about the crops. Bridie looked out the window at the other children, weeding in the sun. She thought about what was going to happen to her. If the Kigleys took her—well, she honestly didn't hold out much hope for them, but it had to be better than the poorhouse. Didn't it?

But there was no *way* she was going to let herself be bound to them. She'd seen it happen to other children in the three months she'd been at the poorhouse, and off they'd gone, willy-nilly. When you were indentured, you didn't get paid a thing until you were twenty-one years old. And you couldn't leave. If you did, they advertised for you in the newspapers and had you sent back.

The thought made Bridie's stomach hurt.

She was alone, and a long way from Ireland.

"Two weeks' trial, then," Mr. Fitch said, and he and Mr. Kigley shook hands.

And Bridie watched as Mrs. Fitch wrote in the ledger, next to Bridie's name:

Taken on trial by Chas. Kigley, June 25, 1848.

Bridie breathed a sigh of relief. She was not to be indentured. Not yet.

2

THE SIGNS ARE NOT PROMISING

Bridie didn't have any things to pack. The poor-house inmates were issued clean clothes every Sunday morning, but they weren't their own clothes. Bridie had only the gray cotton dress she stood up in, an apron, gray stockings, a bonnet, and a pair of laced-up, ankle-high shoes.

The Kigleys' wagon was waiting outside. A dusty horse stood patiently, flicking his ears at flies.

"Now, then, Brigid," said Mr. Fitch, the poor-house keeper.

And Bridie knew what he was going to say, because she'd heard him say it to all the other kids. There was stuff about duty, and remembering that we are put on earth to work hard, and not to become a charge on the county, and that with hard work and obedience she could grow up and become—

Here the lecture changed according to whether you were a boy or girl. If you were a boy you could become all sorts of things, according to Mr. Fitch's lecture. If you were a girl you could merely marry them.

"And above all, remember that you will one day become the mother of citizens of this great Republic," Mr. Fitch finished.

The horse plopped out a pile of steaming manure onto the ground.

"Where am I *going*?" Bridie said.

"Speak when spoken to," snapped Mrs. Fitch.

"To the Kigleys' farm," said Mr. Fitch.

Figured. Farmers needed more help than anyone else. The work was endless.

Suddenly Bridie realized she could be leaving here forever. This could be her last chance to say goodbye.

While Mr. Kigley unhitched the horse from the hitching post, and Mrs. Kigley gathered her skirts to climb into the wagon, Bridie ducked away, ran between the barn and the oven house, and darted around behind the poorhouse to the cemetery.

The graves in the cemetery were unmarked,

mounds subsiding into the rocky New York soil. But Bridie knew which one she was looking for. She ran all the way to the farthest row and the third-to-last grave.

She knelt down and put her hand on it. She felt as if there was something she ought to say, but she couldn't think what it was.

She heard footsteps coming toward her, and she quickly picked up a pebble from the grave and stuck it in her apron pocket, to remember by. Then she looked up and saw Mrs. Fitch coming toward her.

Bridie braced herself in case she was about to get smacked.

But Mrs. Fitch's face risked a bit of sympathy. "Come along, Brigid," she said, not unkindly. "The Kigleys are waiting. Don't give them a bad impression of you."

Too late for that, Bridie thought as she followed Mrs. Fitch back to the wagon.

"After all, it's only for two weeks," said Mrs. Fitch. "Then if they don't find you suit, they'll bring you back and we will try again."

"What if *I* don't find *they* suit?" said Bridie. This was the sort of question that tended to get her into trouble.

"That is not the attitude with which you should

begin," said Mrs. Fitch. "Think of your duty, Brigid. Always, always, think of your duty."

Bridie looked up at Mrs. Fitch and noticed for the first time how tired she looked.

"If you think, every morning upon rising, 'I will do my duty,' and every night, upon retiring, 'I have done my duty,' you will find it a great comfort."

Bridie doubted this very much.

The Kigleys were waiting, looking grim and annoyed. Bridie climbed up into the back of the wagon and sat in the hay.

"Git up, Dobbin," said Mr. Kigley.

The horse flicked his ears, the wagon creaked, and the journey began. Soon they were trotting down the road, and the poorhouse was growing smaller in the distance. Bridie closed one eye, and found she could blot out the poorhouse with her thumb.

Nobody said anything.

The wagon rolled past wheat fields and pastures, and farmhouses with chickens pecking in the dooryard. The sweet smell of milkweed drifted up from the roadside. Bridie began to think the Kigleys were uncommon silent folk. *She* couldn't say anything, of course: she hadn't been spoken to, and anyway she was feeling her way, seeing what these people were like. So far the signs weren't promising.

Still, it was good to be out in the world again, seeing the wide open spaces that this America was made of. She looked back. She could no longer see the poorhouse. She clutched the pebble in her pocket.

She wondered who would be able to manage Mad Janet now.

Bridie knew she could have been sent away before her mother died. She wasn't sure if it was Mrs. Fitch or her husband who had prevented it. There was kindness in the world, after all, even in places where it hardly dared to show its head.

She looked at where the sun was, and figured they were headed north, toward Seneca Falls. Bridie chirked up. Seneca Falls was the mill town where she used to live, with her mother—well, where she'd lived for a little while, anyway. Seneca Falls wasn't the middle of nowhere; it was the middle of everywhere. It had a turnpike and a canal and a railroad.

Starting from Seneca Falls, you could go anywhere in the world.

Sure enough, they were drawing closer to Seneca Falls. Bridie could see the church steeples, and then the tall stone mill where her mother had worked, and then the other mills and the houses.

Then, just as it looked like they were going to

come into the town proper, Dobbin turned at the corner by the American Hotel and headed out of town again.

Bridie's heart sank. Well, of course a farmer wasn't going to live right in town. Maybe they'd be *near* town, anyway.

They passed a schoolhouse, and a big house on a hill where two little white boys were playing in the yard, watched over by a black girl about Bridie's age. No, not *black*, Bridie corrected herself; it was more polite to say *colored* or *a girl of color*.

The children were too far away for Bridie to see clearly. But the older of the little boys waved, and Bridie waved back, and then the girl waved too.

If only Bridie were going to live in *that* house, with those friendly-looking people.

No such luck. The wagon was out of town now, heading down toward the shore of Cayuga Lake.

Dobbin drew to a stop. A wooden tollgate blocked the way.

A woman came out of the stone house beside the gate.

"Two shillings to cross, please," she said.

It had seemed odd to Bridie, when she'd first arrived, that Americans used English money, mixed in with their own.

"But my wagon's empty!" said Mr. Kigley. "We ain't come to trade, we ain't boughten nothing!"

The woman had the air of having heard that before. "A wagon is a wagon."

"But I didn't pay in the morning coming over!"

"No one was at home, so we left the gate up. Now it's two shillings, please."

Mr. Kigley swore.

Bridie was shocked. She'd seen awful things in her life, things so terrible that the nightmares still woke her up with a jolt in the dark. But she had never, ever heard a grown man swear at a woman. It was *illegal* to swear.

Mrs. Kigley looked stricken at what her husband had done. She turned to the tollgate woman. "I'm so s—"

"No one asked you!" Mr. Kigley snarled.

Bridie got to her feet. She had more than half a mind to jump out of the wagon right then. Later she wished she'd done it. But the wagon wheeled around suddenly and she fell down on the boards. Soon they were cantering along toward the free bridge a few miles to the north.

After they crossed, the wagon went on for a couple of hours—no longer at a canter, or even a trot. Dobbin was tired.

How far were they getting from the poorhouse, and from Seneca Falls? Too far, Bridie thought. I should jump out. I should run.

Then the horse turned off the road and up a dirt track. They passed through fields and stopped beside a whitewashed house and barn with a well in the front yard.

And they were home.

3

THE KIGLEY FARM

It didn't feel like home, of course. Home was still Ireland. Home was still a stone cottage, even after the roof had been pulled down by the landlord. Home was with her parents and brothers, making a shelter as best they could of the walls and the open sky. . . .

Bridie blinked back memory. Ireland seemed a lifetime away, though she'd left only a year ago. This was here and now, and she had to be brave and face it.

She was on an American farm, and not a particularly poor one.

There was a small clapboard farmhouse and a barn. Hogs rooted in a farmyard that buzzed with flies. The place smelled overwhelmingly of hog. Chickens pecked and gurgled amongst the hogs. There would never be hunger here, thought Bridie.

But the place felt dangerous, all the same.

It was a long way from anywhere.

She put her hand in her pocket and clutched the pebble from her mother's grave.

"Come in and help me get supper," said Mrs. Kigley, as Mr. Kigley saw to the wagon and Dobbin.

Bridie followed her through the kitchen door. There was a big fireplace with a kettle hanging over top of it. The kitchen smelled of woodsmoke and old onions. There were more flies. It was too warm, but kitchens always were in summer.

A girl came into the kitchen.

Bridie hadn't been expecting that. Well, no one had told her anything. But there she was, the girl, about a year younger than Bridie. She had tight brown braids and a homespun dress and she stared at Bridie as if Bridie were some kind of creature in a circus.

"That's Lavinia," said Mrs. Kigley. "I've had five and she's the only one that lived."

This struck Bridie as an uncomfortable sort

of introduction, but she smiled and tried to look friendly. "How-do-you-do, Lavinia."

Lavinia scowled. "The last orphan we had was prettier than you."

"Lavinia, take Brigid out and get water," said Mrs. Kigley.

Lavinia grabbed two wooden buckets and half gave, half threw one to Bridie.

"No one asked me if I wanted another orphan," said Lavinia as soon as they were outside.

Bridie didn't answer this. Sooner or later she might have to deal with Lavinia, but now was not the time. There was a tarnation uneasy feeling about the Kigley farm. All was not right here.

The well was stone-lined. There was a long wooden lever to raise and lower the bucket. In the next twenty-four hours Bridie came to know the lever and the bucket very well.

Because the next day was wash day. And wash day needed bucket after bucket of water to fill the big copper kettles, to boil the wash.

"You Irish?" said Lavinia as they wrung out Mr. Kigley's shirts.

Bridie nodded.

"I'm American," said Lavinia. "American is better than Irish."

This was certainly not true, but Bridie wasn't

going to get in a fight about it. Not out here in the middle of nowhere, with nobody on her side.

"Was you in the famine?" said Lavinia.

In the famine. As if it was a place people visited. Bridie nodded, briefly, and brushed a fly off her face.

"I heard about them coffin ships," said Lavinia. "Did you come over in one of them?"

Again, a brief nod. Bridie didn't want to think about it, much less talk about it to someone who thought Bridie's life story was some sort of entertainment.

"What was it like?"

"Just a ship," said Bridie.

Lavinia narrowed her eyes, suspecting she wasn't being treated with the honor she was due. "Did your parents die in the famine?"

"Mm-hm," said Bridie. Her father had, anyway. She gathered up a pile of wrung-out shirts and took them over to spread on the ground.

Her father, and her brothers, and now there was only Bridie left.

❧

The Kigleys didn't let Bridie sit at the table with them at meals. She had to wait and eat the leftovers.

19

This didn't bother her. It was a nice change from the long, silent table in the poorhouse, waiting for grace before they were allowed to touch their spoons and then all slurping away at once.

And she was careful to cook enough that there would be plenty left over. She brought up salt pork from the barrels in the cool, earth-smelling cellar. She cooked salt pork with beans, and salt pork with cornmeal, while the flies buzzed around. Sometimes she made hasty pudding.

She cooked potatoes, too. Eating potatoes while people in Ireland were still starving for lack of them made her feel awful.

She didn't mind where she had to sleep; a straw pallet in a corner of the kitchen. She didn't mind that the barn cats sometimes wandered in and shared it with her. She didn't even really mind being awakened by flies crawling on her face. At least, not much.

She didn't mind the work, because it was about the same as the poorhouse in that respect.

No, the thing she minded most was Lavinia.

It started that first day, when they were doing the wash. Bridie went to feel the clothes, to see if they'd dried yet. She found herself grabbing a stiff, child-sized pair of breeches.

She stared at them in dismay. The Kigleys did not have a son. These tiny breeches could only belong to Mr. Kigley, and they had been full-sized going into the wash.

Bridie knew she hadn't thrown these breeches into the boiling water. Lavinia must have done it.

When Lavinia came out to feel the clothes too, a look of sheer terror flew across the girl's face. Bridie felt sorry for Lavinia, for about a second.

Then Lavinia said, "Look what you did! Idiot! You shrank Papa's trousers!"

"I did not! You were the one who put—"

"Mama! The poorhouse girl shrank Papa's trousers!"

Mrs. Kigley came surging out of the house, grabbed Bridie by the arm, seized up the stick used to stir the laundry, and began belaboring Bridie with it.

"I didn't!" Bridie yelled, ducking.

"Do you know how long it took me to card the wool"—SMACK!—"spin the wool"—SMACK!—"weave the cloth"—SMACK!—"sew the—"

"It wasn't me!" Bridie screamed, struggling as the blows rained down on her. "It was Lavinia!"

"It was not! It was not! Liar!" Lavinia danced around the melee.

"Was too!" yelled Bridie.

"You think I'd believe"—SMACK!—"a poorhouse brat"—SMACK!—"over my own daughter?"

Bridie managed to break free. She ran to the barn, where she hid in Dobbin's stall and fumed.

Later, when Mr. Kigley came in from the fields, he saw what had happened to his trousers.

He held up the tiny trousers, his two fingers spreading the waist to the full distance of ten inches or so. And Bridie felt a sudden pang as she thought how her own father would have made a joke of this, would have said they were *bríste* for a leprechaun. He would have waggled his fingers and made the pants dance, and laughed at his loss.

That had been Bridie's father. This was Mr. Kigley.

He threw the ruined trousers aside and reached for a leather strap that hung beside the fireplace. And he turned on his wife. And he raised the strap.

"It wasn't me!" Mrs. Kigley cried, throwing up her arms to protect her head. "It was—"

"IT WASN'T ME!" shrieked Lavinia, and ran out the door as the strap cracked down across her mother's back.

"It was the poorhouse girl!" yelled Mrs. Kigley.

And Mr. Kigley turned on Bridie. The look in his

eyes was terrible, like a mad animal. Bridie curled up into an egg on the hearth, her knees against her chest and her face in her knees, and hugged herself tight and waited for it to be over.

After that, she knew what her real job in the Kigley household was. It was to take the blame.

4

THE LAST STRAW

The next morning, Bridie woke up early. She brushed away the ashes on the banked kitchen fire and blew on the embers until a red glow squirmed through them. She added water to the pot from a bucket she'd brought in last night. She swung the pot across the fire.

Then she went to the door and looked out.

The gray morning mist reminded her of Ireland. There, the potato plants had been planted right across the yard and up to the cottage door. Here, the big vegetable garden was on the other side of the farmyard, behind its wooden fence. Lavinia had weeded it last night, while Bridie was making dinner.

Through the fog she could make out something moving in the vegetable garden. Had some animals gotten through the fence? Or was it birds?

And, by the way, why were there no hogs in the farmyard?

Bridie felt a jolt of alarm.

She ran across the farmyard as fast as she could, her bare feet squelching in the cold mud. The garden gate was open. Her heart sank.

The vegetable garden—what was left of it—was full of hogs.

Bridie yelled at a hog whose mouth was full of turnip greens. It chewed and stared at her. The other hogs went on munching.

Bridie kicked the hog. She shoved. She hollered.

She didn't stop to think that the hogs were bigger than her and could be dangerous. She was only thinking about the vegetables. She knew what could happen to a family whose crops failed.

She rushed around the garden, kicking and yelling and waving her arms, chasing and shoving the hogs toward the garden gate.

"What is the meaning of this!"

Bridie looked up over the rump of a black-and-white-spotted hog she was trying to shove through the gate. She saw Mrs. Kigley, with Lavinia close behind her.

"The hogs got into the garden!" said Bridie, stating the obvious.

"Why did you let them, you fool?"

"I didn't! Lavinia left the—"

"I did not! It was the poorhouse girl!" shrieked Lavinia.

Then Mr. Kigley came running out of the house. Lavinia and Mrs. Kigley took one look at his red, furious face and fled.

That left Bridie, facing a raging Mr. Kigley, with only a hog between them.

Bridie turned and ran across the ruined garden and clambered over the picket fence on the far side. She ran barefoot through the fields until she came to a creek, and then she dived down the bank and peered up, through a clump of tall grass, to see if Mr. Kigley was chasing her.

He wasn't. She stayed there, hiding, and gradually the soft sound of rushing water calmed her down. At last she saw him leave with Dobbin and the wagon . . . going to get more vegetable seeds, maybe.

※

Other things happened in the following days. A rope broke, and one of the firkins of butter cooling in the well fell down and was lost. One of the cats threw up on a wheel of cheese in the cellar. It was always Bridie's fault.

Bridie tried to think what to do. If she ran away to the poorhouse—assuming she could even find her way there—then the Fitches might just send her back here. Children were supposed to expect to be thrashed now and then. Most grown-ups regarded it as a good thing, an important part of a child's education.

Could she get the Fitches to understand that this was different—the maniacal look in Mr. Kigley's eyes, the way his wife and daughter cringed from him, the way they blamed everything on Bridie?

No. Probably not. Mrs. Fitch might understand, if she had the time to listen as she rushed from one duty to another, but Mr. Fitch probably would not, and it would be his opinion that mattered.

At least the Kigleys had only taken Bridie on trial. They'd be taking her back to the poorhouse in another ten days or so. All she had to do was survive until then.

She was lying on her pallet in the kitchen, trying to get to sleep, when she heard Mr. Kigley's voice in the next room.

"Girl's working out pretty well," he said.

Just in a normal tone of voice. Just as if he'd never swung a leather strap at anyone.

"She does as she's told," said Mrs. Kigley.

Nothing about the hogs or the shrunken trousers. Nothing about any of the other things Lavinia had done and then blamed on Bridie.

I bet they *know* it's Lavinia, thought Bridie, infuriated.

"Reckon I'll have her indentured to me," said Mr. Kigley, in a satisfied tone.

Oh, no.

Disaster.

Bridie lay awake for hours, thinking what to do. If she left now, if she ran back to the poorhouse—

Mr. Fitch would say it was good that she was going to be indentured. He would approve. After all, the poorhouse was too crowded as it was. He needed to get her off his hands.

No good.

Then it occurred to her—her indenture would have to be drawn up and signed, wouldn't it? Surely the Kigleys would have to take Bridie along to get the indenture made. And then, in front of the people in the courthouse—would there be a judge?—and Mr. Fitch and everybody, if she absolutely refused, then surely they'd have to listen to her . . . wouldn't they?

This thought kept her going for another two days. Then matters came to a head.

Lavinia broke a dish. And she blamed it on Bridie. And Mrs. Kigley told Mr. Kigley, and he picked up his strap with murder in his eyes, and Bridie ran.

She ran out to the barn, and she ran past Dobbin's stall, and she climbed the ladder into the hayloft and squeezed in among the bales of hay and hid.

She heard the sound of someone coming up the ladder, and she guessed it was Mr. Kigley. She squirmed deeper into the summer-smelling hay. If he pulled the bales away, and found her, she didn't know what she'd do . . . but she wasn't going to let him hit her with that leather strap again. She'd jump out of the hayloft before she'd do that.

She heard him go back down the ladder again. And then she heard the sound of hammering.

She stayed where she was for what seemed like hours. The hay poked through her dress and got in her eyes. Her legs were stiff and cramped from standing perfectly still. There was no sound except for Dobbin stomping in his stall below, and the hum of crickets coming through the wide window of the hayloft.

At last, she crept out from among the hay bales. Flies landed on her. She brushed them away.

She went to the ladder to look down to the barn below.

There were boards nailed across the opening. She couldn't get down the ladder. She was trapped.

5

ACROSS THE LONG BRIDGE

Bridie went to the hayloft window. It wasn't really a window, but more of a wide, open doorway, through which hay was pitched up from the top of a wagon. It was about fifteen feet to the ground.

Too far to jump.

Dusk came creeping in, the late, summer dusk, and then it was night. Bullfrogs croaked and the tiny peeper frogs screeched. When it was too dark for her to be seen, Bridie sat in the doorway and watched the stars spread across the sky, hundreds and then thousands of them, reaching to the far horizon. She tried to think what to do.

The sky clouded over. The stars disappeared, and a soft rain began to fall.

Morning would come, and the Kigleys might let her out, or they might not. Either would be bad.

Her trial period would be up in another week. She might have a chance to get away then. But what if Mr. Kigley killed her before then? That was starting to look like a real possibility. Bridie imagined Mrs. Fitch writing the date of Bridie's death in parentheses in her ledger, and waiting for the ink to dry, and closing the book.

No doubt the sheriff would come out and investigate. There might even be a trial, and Mr. Kigley might hang. That wouldn't do Bridie any good, though.

There was nothing for it. She was going to have to run. And not back to the poorhouse; that would be the first place the Kigleys looked.

She'd go to Seneca Falls, and then she'd figure out what to do. Starting from Seneca Falls, you could go anywhere.

But first she had to get down.

She got armloads of hay, and dropped them into the farmyard below. She hoped this would cushion her fall.

Then she turned around, got down on her hands

and knees, and squirmed backward out the hayloft window. She hung by her hands.

She let go.

Her feet hit the ground so hard her teeth rattled. She fell over backward. The hay hadn't helped at all. She lay still on the ground, the wind knocked out of her.

She got to her feet, shakily. Nothing seemed to be broken.

At least the rain had stopped. The sky had cleared. The moon was a tiny sliver in the sky, but there was light from the stars, and she was able to pick her way along the wagon track, out to the road.

She remembered the way they had brought her. She turned onto the road, and walked until she came to the Turnpike, which was just a dirt road itself, corduroyed with logs in the low, muddy places.

From here she knew her way to Seneca Falls. She knew the Turnpike went straight to the toll bridge— the one that the Kigleys had avoided when they'd brought Bridie home—and then straight into town. All she had to do was follow it.

She made her way past sleeping farms. Some-times dogs barked.

Then a dog came charging at her. She heard its paws scrabbling and its breath as it approached, a dark shadow moving across the ground. Her heart in her mouth, she went on walking. She knew it wouldn't help to run.

The dog came closer. She could see it now, a black shape in the darkness, zooming toward her.

It caught up to her. She froze in terror, unable to move. The dog was huge and menacing. It walked all around her, sniffing.

Bridie waited.

Finally the dog seemed to decide she was no threat. It turned and went home.

Bridie sighed with relief and walked on.

She came into a village. There were no lights burning in the houses, and even the saloon was quiet. It must be very late.

The moon slid behind silver clouds, and the night became darker.

She could smell the lake near at hand. A bullfrog croaked, a sound like a rubber band being twanged. The road sloped down to the lakeshore. The bridge was a dark outline in the night.

She walked up onto the bridge. There was no tollgate at this end. She felt for the wooden railing and walked along beside it, her hand patting the rail instead of sliding so she wouldn't get splinters. She heard the soft knocking of her boots on the bridge's wooden deck, and the lapping of the lake waters against the pilings below.

She'd never been on the Cayuga Lake Bridge before. She'd heard people say it was long. But how long could a bridge be?

A bat plunged at her. She yelped and ducked, then walked on.

Even though she knew the bridge was wide and the railing went the whole way, it made her nervous to be walking on and on and on in the dark over the water. What if there were robbers or murderers hiding in the darkness?

She walked slowly, just in case the bridge suddenly disappeared in front of her. It seemed to her she had been walking for a very long time. The night felt full of terrors. Anything could be in the dark on the bridge here. A big hole, or a gang of evil slave catchers, or a dead body—

Her foot hit something body-like. She yelped.

So did the person she'd just kicked. "Look where you're going, can't you!"

"I can't *see* where I'm going!" said Bridie. Then she added, "I do beg your pardon."

"That's all right, then." The voice sounded a little surprised, as if it wasn't used to having its pardon begged.

It didn't sound like an adult. It sounded like a girl. But it was so dark Bridie couldn't see the stranger at all—they might even be a boy.

"Am I almost at the end of the bridge?" said Bridie.

"Which end?"

That didn't sound encouraging. "The *other* end!"

There was movement in the darkness; the stranger got to their feet. Bridie heard skirts rustling— probably a girl, then. The girl must have been sitting on the edge of the bridge with her legs swinging over the water.

"No, we're right about in the middle here," said the girl.

Her voice didn't come from up above or down below. So the girl must be about the same height as Bridie.

Bridie sighed. "This must be the longest bridge in the world."

"The Ponte Conde de Linhares in India is nearly twice as long," said the girl.

"Oh," said Bridie, not sure how to reply to this. She was not used to people who suddenly started spouting facts about bridges in India.

Anyway, when you are running for your life, you hardly have time to think about such things.

"It might be the second longest, though," said the girl. "It's the longest in the Western Hemisphere. I'm Rose."

Rose's confident tones had the effect of calming Bridie down.

"I'm . . . Bridie," she said. It had just occurred to her that maybe she needed a new name, at least temporarily.

"Are you Irish?"

"Yes," said Bridie, bracing herself for questions about the famine and the coffin ships.

Rose didn't ask them. "Are you running from something?"

Bridie opened her mouth to deny it and heard herself say, "How did you know?"

"It's kind of obvious," said Rose. "I mean, here you are crossing the bridge in the middle of the night. . . ."

"What are *you* doing here?" said Bridie.

"Oh, I come out here for the quiet," said Rose airily, in a tone that made Bridie think she wasn't telling the truth.

Bridie had heard talk, when she'd lived in Seneca Falls last winter. She'd heard about the secret travelers who journeyed the turnpikes and canals of York State, especially at night. . . .

"Are you part of the Underground Railroad?" said Bridie. "Are you waiting for someone? A fugitive?"

Rose didn't say anything, and Bridie added hastily, "I'm, you know, in favor of the Underground Railroad and all."

"I'll walk on with you," said Rose.

They walked along the bridge, Rose in front, Bridie behind, both of them tapping the railing to make sure they were headed the right way.

"Wagons cross this bridge," said Rose, "on the way to Ohio and Missouri and Oregon."

Bridie felt jealous of Rose, who obviously belonged somewhere and mattered enough to maybe be involved in the Underground Railroad. Bridie was acutely aware of not belonging anywhere and not mattering to anybody. She clutched the stone in her pocket.

"Where do you live?" said Rose just then, as if she'd been reading Bridie's mind.

"Oh, just over by . . ." Bridie had been about to give the address in the Flats where she'd boarded with her mother, in those few months before the poorhouse.

Maybe it was because of the darkness, which felt like a safe place for secrets. Maybe it was be-

38

cause Rose hadn't asked about the famine or the coffin ships. Maybe it was because Rose might be an agent of the Underground Railroad, and that meant she was used to keeping secrets. Anyway, Bridie found herself blurting out the whole story. The poorhouse, and the Kigleys, and how Lavinia and Mrs. Kigley blamed everything on Bridie because they were afraid of Mr. Kigley, and everything.

The darkness was loud with crickets, and a fish splashed in the lake below, and Rose listened.

"That doesn't sound good," she said when Bridie had finished. "Well, you'll come home with me tonight, and then . . . what do you need?"

"A job," said Bridie quickly. If she had a job, she could pay for a place to stay; hopefully one where the Kigleys wouldn't look for her. "I'm willing to work, everybody has to."

"I think I can help with that," said Rose. "I know a lady that always needs servants."

"Is she . . ." Bridie trailed off. Rose was being so helpful, and Bridie knew it was rude to ask for even more help, or to be picky.

"The lady is very kind," said Rose. "She's just a little . . ."

"Strange?" Bridie guessed. She didn't mind that.

She could handle strange. She was the best at managing Mad Janet; even Mrs. Fitch admitted that.

"Different," said Rose. "She's different. Do you need a new name?"

"Probably," said Bridie. "At least for a while."

"I'll give you my mother's name," Rose decided. "I don't give it to most people, but I like you."

"Thank you," said Bridie diffidently.

"It was Phoebe."

Was.

Bridie chewed over the name. A phoebe was a bird. In America, girls were named after flowers and birds and even places. During her time in Seneca Falls and the poorhouse, she'd met girls named Indiana and Tennessee, and she'd met two girls named America. Boys mostly had more ordinary names, but she had met a boy named Federal.

"Thank you," she said. Then she added, "Do you name a lot of people?"

"A few. Sometimes when people need to get away, folks come looking for them by their names, you know."

This was apparently as close as Rose was going to get to admitting she was part of the Underground Railroad.

"How did you know that, about the bridge in India?" Bridie asked.

"I read it in a magazine. Shh, we're coming up to the tollhouse."

Bridie didn't know how Rose could tell. "I don't have any money for the toll," she admitted.

"It's okay, they'll be asleep. We just have to slip past. Shh. Take my hand."

Bridie fumbled in the dark and found the outstretched hand. Rose's hand was callused and work-hardened, like Bridie's own.

"Duck," Rose whispered.

Bridie did, but not low enough, and the bar of the tollgate bonked her on the head as they went under it.

"Hey!" a voice called. "Stop here and pay toll!"

Rose and Bridie both started running, hand in hand, their boots slapping the dirt road. Bridie felt suddenly exhilarated and joyful and glad to be alive.

The toll keeper did not give chase, and after a while they stopped running and started walking.

"We'll go to my lodgings," said Rose. "It's down in Seneca Falls and across the river."

"Will your—" There might be a stepmother. "Your parents—"

"My mother's dead and my father's at sea."

Bridie realized she'd told Rose all about herself, but hadn't asked Rose much about *her*self.

"When . . ." Bridie trailed off. She didn't like answering this sort of question herself.

"Two years ago," said Rose.

Bridie waited to see if Rose would say more. But Rose didn't seem to want to, and Bridie could understand that.

Suddenly Bridie found she was too tired to talk, too tired to do anything but keep walking. They crossed the bridge over the Seneca River in silence, except for the rushing of the waterfalls down below. And they came into Seneca Falls.

6

THE STRANGE MRS. STANTON

When Bridie awoke the next morning, she was lying on a straw mattress in an over-warm attic room. She could see nails from the roof shingles poking through the wood beside her.

There was a colored girl about her own age looking down at her.

Bridie had seen this girl around, when she'd briefly lived in Seneca Falls before. Sometimes the girl was hurrying to school, carrying books, and sometimes she was making deliveries, carrying piles of laundry or stacks of half-finished clothes from the mills to be finished by outworkers.

"I thought you'd never wake up," said the girl.

Bridie blinked. She remembered what had happened last night. "Where's Rose?"

"I'm Rose," said the girl.

"Oh," said Bridie.

She was startled. She had just assumed the girl she'd met on the bridge was white like her.

"Come on downstairs. Breakfast is almost over," said Rose.

Bridie put on her shoes, shook her dress out—she had slept in her clothes—and followed Rose downstairs.

There was a long boarding-house table, half empty. A couple of men, a young woman, and a small boy were still eating. The little boy stared at Bridie, who was feeling very self-conscious. She'd never been the only white person in the room before.

The adults did not stare, but one man said solemnly, "Rose, I don't know how to tell you this, but that is not an Underground Railroad passenger."

"Oh, leave her alone, Frank," called a voice from the kitchen. A young colored man stuck his head into the room, looked at Bridie, and smiled. "Are you hungry?"

"Yes, please," said Bridie.

"Thank you, Mr. Moody," said Rose. "I'll pay for—"

"No, you won't!" Mr. Moody shook his spoon at her. "I'm not so poor I can't afford to give a guest breakfast."

And two minutes later Bridie was sitting next to Rose at the table, with a stack of flapjacks in front of her, with butter *and* maple syrup.

She was so hungry she started eating without even waiting for grace. She stopped guiltily while Rose said grace, then she started up again. She'd only had maple syrup a couple of times before, and she was very much in favor of it.

The other people at the table got up and left one by one, on their way to work, Bridie supposed. Work. She needed work. She wondered about the woman Rose had said might hire her.

Rose had said the woman was a little different. In Bridie's experience, when people said that, they usually meant the person was a *lot* different.

Bridie helped Rose clear the table, plunging the dishes into a wooden washtub.

"No canal run, Mr. Moody?" Rose asked.

"Not on the Erie. Just a short run down the Cayuga & Seneca last night, and now I'm off for a few days. That's why there's flapjacks." He looked at Bridie, then at Rose.

Bridie started washing the dishes. She couldn't pay Mr. Moody for the food, so at least she could help with that. She heard Mr. Moody and Rose having a quiet, muttered conversation.

She thought about the Kigleys. She didn't think the Fitches would come looking for her. One less child in the poorhouse would be a good thing as far as they were concerned. But the Kigleys might.

She hoped she could get the job, and that it would enable her to keep out of the Kigleys' sight.

Rose went upstairs, and came down with a stack of small, leather-bound schoolbooks.

"I go to school over there by Locust Hill," she explained. "Right by Mrs. Stanton's house. I'll take you there first."

As they left the house, Bridie looked up State Street toward the railroad tracks. There was a schoolhouse right there. Bridie had gone to it herself for a couple of weeks last winter, before Mama got really sick and before the poorhouse and all that.

"Why don't you go to that school?" Bridie asked, pointing.

"Because the teacher doesn't want colored children," said Rose.

"Oh." Now that Bridie thought about it, there hadn't been any colored children there. Even though most of the colored families in Seneca Falls lived right on State Street.

She felt guilty for having been so wrapped up in her own troubles that she hadn't even thought about those of her new friend. "Has your father been at sea long?" she asked.

"Yes," said Rose. "He was a boatman on the Erie Canal, but then he had an offer of work on a whaling vessel and . . . that's the last we heard of him."

"Oh." Bridie didn't know what to say. "When was that?"

They crossed busy Fall Street with its shops and factories, and started down the steep slope of Water Street to the bridge.

"Three years ago," said Rose. "Before Mama died."

"But, you know, three years, that's not really long at all for a whaling voyage, and if the ship had gone down there'd be news of it by now, and . . ."

Bridie knew she was babbling, even before Rose gave her a look.

"Sometimes colored sailors disappear even when the ship doesn't go down," said Rose. "They get *sold*."

"Oh." Bridie tried to think of something comforting to say to this, and couldn't.

They were on the bridge crossing the Seneca River now. Bridie could hear the rushing of the man-made waterfalls that powered the factories. She looked downstream toward the islands called the Flats, where she and her mother had had lodgings last fall and winter. It seemed like forever ago.

Mules on the towpath hauled barges away from the factories, taking all the things that were made in Seneca Falls out toward the Erie Canal and the world.

"But letters get misdirected a lot too," said Bridie.

"That's true," said Rose. "And sometimes they just take ages to arrive."

They walked along Bayard Street. . . . They were going back the way they'd come last night. This made Bridie nervous. What if this Mrs. Stanton knew the Kigleys?

"Um, if this lady lives out the way—"

"She's right at the edge of town," said Rose. "Not much further now."

They passed houses and stores and the American Hotel. They picked their way through a herd of mooing cows coming the other way. Even with the warm, friendly smell of cattle all around her, Bridie was getting nervous.

"What if the lady doesn't like me?"

"Then she'll probably hire you anyway," said Rose. "But don't worry! Why wouldn't she like you?"

They turned down Washington Street, passing

a schoolhouse. This must be where Rose went to school.

Bridie could hear the sound of a sawmill, and the calls of boatmen on the canal. There was a big house on a rise above the road.

Suddenly Bridie knew where she was. Just across the rickety, narrow catwalk bridge was the part of the Flats where she and her mother had stayed. And here, on this side of the canal . . . She recognized the big white house. She'd seen it from the Turnpike the day the Kigleys had picked her up at the poorhouse. And there had been two little boys playing in the yard, and—

"I saw you here!" said Bridie. "The day they took me out to the farm."

She remembered the children on the lawn. They'd been too far away to recognize, but now she was sure the girl had been Rose.

"Sometimes I work for Mrs. Stanton, and sometimes she lets me read her books," said Rose.

They climbed a set of wooden steps from the road up to the yard. There was a metal boot scraper beside the porch, and they stopped to scrape the mud and manure from the streets off their shoes.

"If this doesn't work out, come and find me," said Rose. "We'll think of something else."

Bridie felt instantly less worried. She could count

on Rose even if Mrs. Stanton wouldn't hire her. It was something she'd learned as a small child back in Ireland: the poor were more likely to help each other than the rich were to help anybody.

Rose led the way up onto the porch, and knocked.

There was a sound of footsteps within. The door opened, and a white woman stood there. She had a dishrag in her hand. A boy about four years old was clinging to her voluminous skirts.

"Good morning, Mrs. Stanton," said Rose.

"Well, good morning, Rose." Mrs. Stanton looked harried, as if her mind were on other things. "What brings you here?"

"My friend Br—er, Phoebe is looking for work," said Rose.

Mrs. Stanton looked at Bridie with interest. "And what timing. My cook has gone to care for her sick mother, and Evangeline has alas gone to a better place."

"I didn't know Evangeline died," said Rose.

"Did I say she died? She moved to Boston. Can you mind children, Phoebe?"

"Yes, ma'am," said Bridie. "And I can cook a bit, and clean."

"Really clean? Tell me how you clean."

"Well, um, sweep and mop and scrub the floors, and dust, and . . ."

"That will do to begin with," said Mrs. Stanton. "You sound Irish, which makes Phoebe a rather surprising name for you."

Mrs. Stanton was uncommon sharp. Bridie and Rose exchanged a glance. "Yes, ma'am," said Bridie.

"I have no prejudice against hiring the Irish," said Mrs. Stanton. "Provided they're diligent and sober. Won't you come in?"

Just then, a boy about six years old came charging toward the doorway, dodging around Mrs. Stanton, who caught him by the arm and inspected him.

"Comb hair, wash hands." She turned him around and gave him a gentle shove back into the house.

"I want to go to school too!" said the smaller boy hanging on to her skirt.

"You're not old enough, Kit."

In the distance, the school bell clanged.

"Oh, Neil, you'll be late!" Mrs. Stanton hurried into the house, leaving the door open and taking the dishrag and Kit with her.

"I have to go," said Rose. "But I'll see you later."

"Thank you," said Bridie.

Rose hurried off down the hill with her books. Bridie stood, uncertain, on the porch. Was she supposed to go in?

51

Mrs. Stanton reappeared, looking even more harried, and pushing Neil ahead of her. Neil was carrying his schoolbooks buckled onto the end of a long book strap. Bridie envied him the book strap; only boys were allowed to have them. He broke away from his mother and ran down the hill, swinging his books round and round over his head.

"Oh dear. If he lets go he could hurt somebody," said Mrs. Stanton. Then she brightened. "Well, that's how we learn. Do come in, Phoebe."

Bridie stepped into Mrs. Stanton's parlor and tried not to stare.

She had never in her life been in a house as nice as this one. There was *wallpaper*. There was a writing desk, and a piano, and all sorts of things that were a world away from her family's cottage in Ireland (before the landlord had it pulled down), and Bridie and her mother's lodgings down in the Flats, and the whitewashed poorhouse walls with stern black mottoes painted on them.

And there were books. Lots of books. Bridie had never seen so many books ever.

"You'll notice there are no carpets," said Mrs. Stanton. "Too much work to clean, and anyway I believe they trap mold and spread disease. You've a good head. Do you mind if I assess your organs?"

Bridie reminded herself that Rose had said Mrs. Stanton was kind, but different. "My what?"

"You are familiar with phrenology? I do like to take a scientific approach to hiring household help."

Oh. Science. That was all right, then. Besides, Bridie had never had her bumps read, and she was curious as to what they would say. "Yes, ma'am."

She untied her bonnet.

There came a loud banging sound from the back of the house, where Bridie supposed the kitchen must be.

Mrs. Stanton ignored the noise and began running her hands over Bridie's head. Bridie felt fingers poking and probing through her hair.

"Hmm. Interesting." Mrs. Stanton said this several times as she felt the back of Bridie's head, and the top of her head, and the sides, and peered at her eyes and forehead and ears. "Interesting."

Bridie couldn't tell whether it was the good kind of interesting or the bad kind.

"I'll work hard!" she burst out, unable to take this any longer.

Mrs. Stanton dropped her hands and looked surprised. "You've a good head, really. An excellent bump of causality, which means you can understand first principles and can reason. And you've a very large friendship bump. You must make friends easily."

"Yes, ma'am." Bridie didn't stop to think about whether all this was true or not; she was too worried about getting the job.

"Your bump of cautiousness is, I'm afraid, hardly there at all. In fact, I would call it more of a hollow. But, with care, perhaps you can develop it."

Bridie thought of all those times she'd ended up locked in the cell at the poorhouse. She wasn't surprised to hear she lacked a bump of cautiousness.

BANG-BANG-BANG from the kitchen.

"What about school?" Mrs. Stanton asked her. "Don't you attend the summer term?"

"No, ma'am. I've my living to get."

"So has Rose, but she manages. Can you read, write, and do arithmetic?"

"Read and write, yes. . . . I'm a *girl*, ma'am."

"And that's an excuse for not learning arithmetic? *I* learned it, and geometry, too."

Bridie said nothing. She needed to grow her bump of cautiousness, and Mrs. Stanton hadn't said she'd hire Bridie yet. The poorhouse didn't teach arithmetic to girls, and Bridie didn't see why Mrs. Stanton should blame *her* for it.

The banging sound grew louder. Mrs. Stanton

led the way back to the kitchen, where small Kit was whacking on a brass kettle with a spoon.

"Do stop that, dear," said Mrs. Stanton, taking the spoon from him.

There was a modern wood-burning cookstove in the kitchen, Bridie saw. These were new and rare contraptions. She'd have to learn to use it.

"The baby's having his nap," said Mrs. Stanton. "I have three boys: Daniel, whom we call Neil, and Henry, whom we call Kit, and Gerrit, whom we call Gat. I do not frighten them with stories of the devil or hell, nor do I permit anyone else to do so. Are you looking for a live-in job?"

"Yes, ma'am," said Bridie. That would solve her problem of a place to stay. And it might help her hide . . . although she didn't like how this place was so close to the Turnpike. The Kigleys might come rolling along at any moment. Still, from up here on the hill, she might see them coming.

"A grown serving woman is paid a dollar a week," said Mrs. Stanton. "A girl your age not half as much—two shillings at most."

Bridie didn't bother trying to work out the difference. "Yes, ma'am."

"It is not nearly enough," said Mrs. Stanton.

Bridie yes-ma'amed again.

"The toil is endless," said Mrs. Stanton.

This did not sound promising.

"A man can work half as hard as a woman and be paid twice as much," said Mrs. Stanton, swinging the spoon she'd taken from the child, thoughtfully.

Rose had been right. Mrs. Stanton was a bit different.

Little Kit, meanwhile, had wandered outside—the screen door banged shut.

"I shall pay you a dollar a week, as I would a grown woman," Mrs. Stanton decided. "But I will expect you to work for it."

"Yes, ma'am. Thank you, ma'am." Bridie felt a mix of relief and alarm.

"Can you start today? That is, as soon as you've gone home and gotten your things? And will I be paying you, or your parents?"

"I don't have any things," said Bridie. "Or any parents."

"Maybe you'd better tell me the whole story, Phoebe. Have you run away from home?" Mrs. Stanton looked at Bridie with sharp, searching eyes.

And you could see in those eyes that Mrs. Stanton was tarnation clever. She'd probably read all those books in the parlor. And some of them, Bridie had noticed, weren't even in English.

Bridie felt cornered. "Not from home, no."

"Then from . . . ?"

"The Kigleys," said Bridie, giving up.

The screen door banged as small Kit came back inside.

"Your former employers?"

"Not exactly, no. They took me on trial. I was to be bound to them."

"But you weren't bound yet?"

"No, ma'am."

"And why did you leave them?"

Bridie wasn't sure what to say. If she said she'd been beaten, that might make Mrs. Stanton figure Bridie was a bad worker, in spite of having mostly-good bumps on her head.

"Were they unkind?"

That was a good way of putting it. Bridie nodded.

There was a series of loud clangs. Kit had picked up the brass kettle and was dropping it on the floor to see how high he could make it bounce.

Mrs. Stanton took the kettle away from him. "Kit, go upstairs and see if your brother is awake." She turned back to Bridie. "Did they beat you, beyond the moderate correction permitted by the law?"

"I guess probably." Bridie didn't know much

about the law, but she knew that if she'd stayed, the Kigleys would have killed her. "I guess definitely."

"Then you had every right to leave them," said Mrs. Stanton. "The statute is somewhat vague on this point, but the courts are not. You need have no fear at all, Phoebe. I have studied the law and know this."

"Yes, ma'am," said Bridie. "I don't think the Kigleys have studied the law, though, and I don't suppose they know."

She snapped her mouth shut as if she could put the words back in. That was sassin' and talking back and how Bridie had gotten locked in that cell so many times.

Mrs. Stanton, however, gave Bridie an assessing look and a smile.

Kit came into the kitchen. "He's awake, Mama."

"I'll go see to him." Mrs. Stanton turned to Bridie. "He has fever-and-ague, and I'm treating it homeopathically, which I must say doesn't seem to be working very well. Have you had it yet?"

"Yes, ma'am." Everyone in Seneca Falls, it seemed, had to go through fever-and-ague, which some people called *malaria* because it was thought to be caused by bad air.

"There are beans in the bin there," said Mrs.

Stanton. "Take out two measures and pick through them, then start them on the fire to soak."

And she left, and Bridie looked at the stove. With her bump of causality, she should be able to figure it out.

7

THE SCHOOL AT LOCUST HILL

Rose arrived at school and sat at the back, as she'd been told to. There were a couple of other colored children in the little one-room school, but they were boys, so they sat on the other side of the room—also in the back.

This wasn't exactly a rule, but Mr. Davis had said it would be best. If a parent complained about the children of color, then the children would have to leave. There was no law saying they couldn't be in school, but there was also no law saying they could.

Mr. Davis called the first class up to recite: the

ones in the primer. Mrs. Stanton's son Neil was in that class. But Rose wasn't, so she sat and flipped through her newest book and waited for her class to be called. She knew it was going to be an uncomfortable lesson.

Summer-smelling air wafted through the open windows. Rose could hear horses passing on the road, and the distant whine of the sawmill.

Her new book was a common school arithmetic. The clerk at Hoskins's store had given her a funny look when she'd bought it, and she hoped it wasn't going to be eight cents wasted. But she'd thought long and hard before she'd plunked down that eight cents on the counter.

"Third Reader," called Mr. Davis, and with a sigh Rose stood up.

She marched to the front of the class and lined up beside Mr. Davis's desk with two other girls and one boy. She stood all the way on the right, as if she were at the bottom of the class, which she was not. Some days, she was at the top of the class, but Mr. Davis always put her at the bottom anyway.

He always seemed to be fretting about that one white parent who might complain.

"We shall read the dialogue on page one hundred ninety-four," said Mr. Davis.

The students obediently opened their *New York Reader No. 3* to page 194.

She hoped he wouldn't call on her. He never called on her. Why should he call on her today?

"James and Rose," said Mr. Davis.

He'd called on her.

"Which part do I read, please?" said Rose.

Mr. Davis gave her an I-don't-have-time-for-this look. "The slave, Rose."

Like she didn't know.

James cleared his throat and began. "'Now, vill . . . villain! What have you to say for this second att . . .'" He cast an agonized look at Mr. Davis.

"Attempt," said Mr. Davis.

"'. . . Attempt to run away?'"

"'I well know that nothing I can say will avail,'" said Rose resignedly. "'I submit to my fate.'"

Rose had never been enslaved. Neither had her parents. New York had abolished slavery in 1827, and anyone born in the state after July 4, 1799, was born free.

But it wasn't like she didn't think about slavery every day, and the millions of people that were still prisoners to it. She carried on reading.

James was halting and stumbling. It was clear he hadn't read over his lesson, and Mr. Davis was giving him a hard look. With extreme difficulty, James asked Rose what she had to say for herself.

She clenched her teeth and read aloud, "'I am a slave, that is answer enough.'"

James, with some prompting from Mr. Davis on the hard words, asked Rose if she didn't think she'd been treated humanely.

"'Humane!'" Unlike James, Rose *had* read over the lesson, and her voice rang out across the schoolhouse. "'Does it deserve that appellation to keep your fellow men in forced subjection, deprived of all exercise of the free will, liable to all the injuries that your own caprice or the brutality of your overseers may heap on them? Look at these limbs! Are they not those of a man?!'"

Several students giggled. Mr. Davis gave them a look. "Quietly, Rose."

"'Think that I have the spirit of a man too!'" said Rose, not quite as loudly.

Someone was still snickering. Mr. Davis reached for his hickory stick, and the laughter quickly subsided. There was an unspoken understanding in the schoolhouse that as long as silence fell the moment Mr. Davis reached for the stick, he would never actually use it.

Rose could feel her face burning. She looked at

Mr. Davis, and he looked back at her. She knew she had read well. She knew she deserved to go to the head of the class, and Mr. Davis surely knew it too.

Besides, it would be some compensation for being made to read the part of the slave.

"James," said Mr. Davis, "you have obviously not prepared at all."

"We had to cut firewood," said James. "And my father was sick."

"Go to the bottom of the class," said Mr. Davis.

Dejectedly, James went and stood to Rose's left.

"I said to the *bottom*."

James moved over to Rose's right, mutely furious.

And that was it. Rose was not moved to the head of the class.

"Class dismissed. Fourth Reader," called Mr. Davis.

As Rose made her way down the aisle, a white boy grinned at her and said quietly but in a high falsetto, "'I am a slave, that is answer enough!'"

Overwhelmed by circumstances, Rose smacked him on the head with her book.

Fortunately, Mr. Davis was busy with the Fourth Reader and didn't notice. Rose went fuming to her seat.

After school, as the students filed out, Rose took a deep breath, gathered her books, and approached the teacher's desk.

Mr. Davis looked up warily. "Yes, Rose? You read very well today."

"Thank you, teacher." Rose guessed that Mr. Davis thought she was going to ask why she hadn't been made head of the class. Rose was not going to ask that. A teacher's decisions were final and any fool knew it.

She put her books down and opened the new one. It smelled of fresh paper and ink and its smooth leather binding. She took a deep breath, mentally crossed her fingers for luck, and said, "I bought an arithmetic, Mr. Davis."

She handed it to him. He took it and riffled through the crisp new pages. "Don't you already know this stuff, Rose?"

He was looking at the early pages, counting and simple addition. The baby stuff. Even girls were taught that, but they didn't usually bother to buy a book for it.

"I know that part, teacher, but . . ."

Gently she took the book from him and opened it to the middle. "I don't understand this part. I read it twice, but I don't understand it."

She had a good head for figures, she knew. But this stuff was new and complicated.

"Well, that's for boys, Rose."

"It doesn't say so." Rose wished the words back as soon as she said them. She'd meant to be polite, but today had been just too much . . . today.

"Rose, you don't need to learn all this. Look, gills and furlongs? Pounds and shillings and dollars and cents? This is for men, who have to deal with business and farming matters. Your husband will take care of all that."

Rose had prepared for this. She flipped open another of her schoolbooks, called *The Brief Remarker on the Ways of Man*. Fortunately it fell open to the page she wanted; Mr. Davis was gathering up his books and things and was clearly ready to leave.

"Listen to this, Mr. Davis. Please," she added. She took a deep breath and read declaimingly, " 'The sexes are equal as to mental powers!' "

You weren't supposed to talk about what was in the lessons; you certainly weren't supposed to argue about them. You read your lessons aloud when you were called on, and if there were questions in the book, you memorized the answers, which were also in the book, and repeated them word-for-word. That was *school*. Mr. Davis gave her a look that plainly said he wasn't being paid enough for this.

"Read the whole sentence, Rose."

Rose had been hoping he wouldn't remember the whole sentence. "'Admitting—whatever be the real fact—that the sexes are equal as to mental powers, it is evident that their destinations are different.'"

"The essay, as I'm sure you know, Rose, argues that girls should *not* have the same education as boys."

"I think the book is wrong, teacher."

As soon as the words were out of her mouth, Rose feared she had gone too far.

Mr. Davis looked at her, exasperated. Rose realized that her audacity could hurt the other students of color as well—and Mr. Davis was the only teacher who'd agreed to teach them.

"Perhaps you should write a book of your own that sets everything right, then."

"I don't want to write a book." There was no going back now, so she plunged on. "I want to be a scientist."

Mr. Davis pinched the top of his nose, like he was getting one of his headaches. "Rose . . ."

"I need to learn arithmetic. Mrs. Stanton up on the hill learned arithmetic all the way to the end of the book like the boys," said Rose. "And *then* she learned geometry."

"Mrs. Stanton up on the hill is the daughter of

a wealthy and famous judge," said Mr. Davis. "I doubt any parents complained. If I were to put you in the higher arithmetic class, the only girl, and colored at that . . ."

Those everlasting parents who might complain. Rose wished all those complaining parents to perdition.

But she sensed that Mr. Davis was about to give in. She waited hopefully.

"Five minutes," he said at last. "I can spare five minutes after school every day to hear your arithmetic lesson."

"Thank you, Mr. Davis!"

"But if you ever, for one day, don't study your lesson, then I will no longer be able to spare five minutes."

Rose felt a surge of delight at her victory. Today was turning out to be all right after all. She wanted to run out of the school into the sunshine, she wanted to go tell her new friend Bridie about her victory.

But she had a shrewd suspicion that James would be lurking outside, waiting to take revenge on her because *he* hadn't prepared his lesson.

And she was right. He was. As soon as he saw her, he scooped up a handful of horse manure from the road. He was just about to hurl it at her when he saw Mr. Davis emerge behind her.

Rose waited while Mr. Davis locked the schoolhouse door. There was nothing James could do. Rose walked on with Mr. Davis, leaving James standing there with horse manure in his hand.

8

THE GLORIOUS FOURTH

On the Fourth of July, the firecrackers started going off just after midnight. Bridie fell asleep in the spaces between explosions until dawn.

By the time she got up to make breakfast, six-year-old Neil was already awake and looking for something to eat. He cut some bread from a loaf while Bridie stirred the fire to life in the stove.

Bridie saw him opening the door to the pie safe.

"Leave all that," she said. "It's for the picnic."

Neil ran out the door before Bridie could tell him he was supposed to take Kit with him, or ask him to go get water. So she had to go out to the pump herself.

Four-year-old Kit came downstairs. He was hopping up and down with excitement—after all, the Glorious Fourth was the most important holiday of the year in this young country. He wanted to go out and watch the militia get ready to parade. Bridie knew that Mrs. Stanton didn't like him crossing the Seneca River by himself. She hung on to him by main force while she stirred the hasty pudding.

Mrs. Stanton finally appeared with Gat, who was mostly over his fever-and-ague for now . . . though it would come back, Bridie supposed. It generally did.

They went out into the yard after breakfast. There was a good view of the river from there. They watched the parade as it made its way up the far side of the river toward the bridge. The militiamen marched, and there were men carrying flags, and men riding horses caparisoned in red, white, and blue, and men in the band, playing stirring marches.

"Is this your first Fourth of July, Phoebe?" asked Mrs. Stanton.

"Yes, ma'am. More or less. Last year we—I was at Grosse Isle in Quebec. In quarantine."

"I want to be in the parade!" said Kit. He marched up and down the yard. Then the screen door banged as he went into the kitchen—to get a pot to use as a drum, Bridie supposed.

"Horseys," said Gat, but not with much spirit; he was still tired from the fever-and-ague.

The parade had reached the bridge and was crossing the river, drums rat-a-tat-tatting.

"Look at them, the lords of creation," said Mrs. Stanton, gesturing at the parade. "You would think the Fourth of July belonged to them, and only them. You'll never see a woman in a parade."

"Yes, ma'am. There are no colored people either," said Bridie.

She'd been hoping that she and Rose could spend the holiday together. But Rose had told her that some of the white men, once they got drunk, took off after the colored people like it was 1776 and they were the British or something. It was not safe for Rose to be seen.

Not much of a holiday, then.

"Well, the parade's gotten to the apple orchard," said Mrs. Stanton. "Shall we go to the speechifying? Oh, you need something red, white, and blue, Phoebe. Just a moment."

Mrs. Stanton went to her sewing basket and found red and blue ribbons, which she laced through Bridie's white bonnet. "There. Pretty, but not gaudy, as the devil said when he painted his tail pea-green."

The day was already hot, and Bridie was grateful she didn't have to dress like Mrs. Stanton, who was wearing many layers of petticoats that made her enormous long skirt stand out stiffly. They headed down the hill.

Bridie carried the picnic basket and Mrs. Stanton held on to the boys as they started off down Bayard Street to Ansel Bascom's orchard.

The whole town seemed to be there. Farm families had come in from the countryside in wagons. Children chased each other among the old gnarled apple trees. Firecrackers were going off everywhere, startling the horses and startling Bridie, too. The air smelled of gunpowder.

Mrs. Stanton winced at every loud bang. "I hate those things. And it is illegal to set them off in town."

Everyone was breaking the law merrily.

People were greeting each other, gathering in clumps, exchanging news.

Kit went off to watch some bigger boys set off fireworks. Mrs. Stanton turned to greet some people she knew. Bridie set the picnic basket down under an apple tree and sat on the lowest branch and felt all alone in the world. Alone and a long way from Ireland. She wished Rose had been able to come.

But no colored folks were there, out of all that lived in Seneca Falls and the country round it.

The militia band was playing in the orchard, and more firecrackers were going off.

Mrs. Stanton was talking to a tiny, elderly-looking lady in a lace bonnet.

"How lovely to see thee again, Lizzie," said the tiny woman. "And is dear Henry here as well?"

Bridie figured the lady must be a Quaker, since she said *thee*.

"No, he's off organizing for the Free Soil Party," said Mrs. Stanton flatly.

"Well, thee knows it is important work," said the lady. "With all the new territories we've suddenly acquired from Mexico—I say nothing of *how* we acquired them—we must do all we can to prevent slavery from being allowed to spread."

"If women could vote, slavery would have ended long ago," said Mrs. Stanton.

"Thee will make us ridiculous, harping on that," said the lady. "I agree women's rights are in a sorry state, but to *vote*—"

"Frederick Douglass agrees with me," said Mrs. Stanton, with a note of finality.

"But Mr. Stanton doesn't, I'll wager."

Bridie had thought at first that there *was* no Mr.

Stanton, but later she'd figured out that there was and that he was never home. His work had to do with abolishing slavery, and he had to travel all over for it.

"I am not beholden to Mr. Stanton for my opinions," said Mrs. Stanton. "When the party coach comes down the road on Election Day, decked out with pine boughs and red, white, and blue ribbons, *I'd* like to be the one jumping in and riding to the polls to vote."

"Sometimes, Lizzie," said the tiny lady, "I think thee takes a stance just to be contrary."

Bridie noticed four-year-old Kit climbing high in an apple tree, holding a firecracker. He probably shouldn't do that, but then again, it didn't appear to be lit.

Still, she'd better make sure. She got out of her tree and went over and made Kit drop the firecracker down to her. It wasn't lit. She stuck it in her apron pocket. It snicked against the pebble she always kept there.

"I do envy you your cotton dress, Phoebe," said Mrs. Stanton, as Bridie made her way back. "So much nicer on these hot days than linen or wool."

"Now, Lizzie, thee knows we mustn't wear cotton," said the lady beside her.

"I know, Lucretia. It's grown by slaves," said Mrs. Stanton fretfully. "Don't think I don't hear about this all the time from Henry. Mrs. Mott, this is my new girl, Phoebe."

"How do you do, Phoebe," said Mrs. Mott.

Bridie curtsied. "How do you do."

The band stopped playing. Through the apple boughs Bridie could see a podium draped in red, white, and blue bunting. A man climbed up to the podium and began to speak. A firecracker exploded. There was a wild neigh of frightened horses, and a scream—someone must have gotten burned.

Bridie climbed back into her tree. She was glad she'd taken the firecracker away from little Kit.

"And so America is seventy-two years old today," said Mrs. Stanton. "Seventy-two years ago this land was all wilderness. I wonder what will come when seventy-two years have passed again?"

"It was not wilderness, Lizzie," Mrs. Mott remonstrated. "The Cayuga Indians farmed it. They planted this very orchard."

"Mrs. Mott has just come from visiting the Cayuga Indians, Phoebe," said Mrs. Stanton, turning and looking up at Bridie.

"Helping them fight to keep what land they do have left," said Mrs. Mott with a sniff.

The man at the podium finished speaking. There were cheers and applause. Bridie, who hadn't really been listening, politely applauded too. Another man came up to the podium and started speaking.

The men speaking used lots of big words. Most people didn't consider a speech any good if it didn't have plenty of big words in it. The speakers talked about the American Revolution and defeating the British. As an Irishwoman, Bridie appreciated this.

"If I had your skill at speechifying, Lucretia, I'd tell these lords of creation such a story," said Mrs. Stanton with a sigh.

"About the usual topic, I suppose?" said Mrs. Mott.

"It's important, Lucretia! Do you know—"

"Oh yes, I know."

The two women went on talking. Bridie listened. They'd both been to England, for an anti-slavery convention, and Mrs. Mott had been a delegate but they hadn't let her take her seat because she was a woman. There were other women delegates too, and they were all made to sit behind a curtain and keep silent while the men talked and voted. It still rankled, apparently, although it had been years ago.

Years ago, when Bridie's parents and brothers

were still alive. Years ago, before the potatoes turned black and burst.

The two women talked about women's rights and about something called "human rights," which Bridie had never heard of before. Anyway, it had nothing to do with her.

A speech ended. Another man came to the podium.

"That's Amelia Bloomer's husband," said Mrs. Stanton to her friend. "You don't know her, but I've been trying to get her interested—"

"'WHEN IN THE COURSE OF HUMAN EVENTS,'" boomed the man at the podium. He had a loud, carrying voice.

Bridie mouthed the words. The Declaration of Independence had been in her reader, back at the poorhouse. She'd had to memorize it, of course. *When in the course of human events . . .*

Mrs. Stanton murmured the words too. "'When in the course of human events . . .'"

Bridie looked at the other girls in the crowd. You could tell which girls came from rich families because they were wearing ankle-length pantalets with white ruffles. Some had even threaded red and blue ribbons through the lace on their ruffles. The poorer girls, like Bridie, just had stockings.

And girls who worked in the mills had stockings, and girls from the farm families—really it was more stockings than ruffles. Take that girl there, for example—

With a start of horror, Bridie realized that she was looking at Lavinia Kigley.

The Kigleys were here.

Mrs. Stanton could say what she liked about the law, but it didn't stop people from setting off firecrackers, and Bridie very much doubted that it would stop the Kigleys from dragging her back to their farm.

She climbed higher up in the apple tree, until she was hidden among the leaves and little green apples, and stayed there until it was time for lunch.

Mrs. Stanton opened the picnic basket, and Bridie—after looking all around for the Kigleys—helped her spread a red-and-white-checked tablecloth on the ground. The boys came running back, smelling strongly of firecrackers.

Bridie kept low to the ground so that she could hide behind the others—she didn't know where the Kigleys were now, but she didn't intend to let them see her.

Mrs. Mott helped Mrs. Stanton set out the food. There were egg and cheese sandwiches, and canned sardines from France, and two jars of pickles. But the crowning glory of the picnic was the pies. Gooseberry tart, and dried-apple pie, and pigeon pie, and blackberry pie, and coconut custard pie.

Bridie had never seen such a feast in her life. She clutched the stone in her pocket and wished her mother could have been there.

Everyone took a plate and started looking over the food, choosing what they wanted.

"Help yourself, Phoebe," Mrs. Stanton urged.

"Yes, do eat, Phoebe," said Mrs. Mott, handing her an empty plate. "Thee is much too thin."

That's right, Bridie thought. She was *Phoebe*. And if Bridie couldn't join a feast while people were starving back home, Phoebe surely could. She started filling her plate. Maybe she would be able to eat a slice of each kind of pie, if she skipped the sandwiches.

She took a bite of the coconut pie, savoring the smooth custard and the strange taste of coconut. She wished Rose could have been there.

Meanwhile, Mrs. Stanton and Mrs. Mott were still talking about human rights, which had nothing to do with Bridie.

9

A TEA PARTY AT WATERLOO

In the days following the Fourth of July, Bridie kept a weather eye out for Kigleys. She watched the Turnpike, from her vantage point on Locust Hill, while she pumped water. The days were getting hot, and she let the cold water overflow from the bucket onto her bare toes.

Sometimes the rain came crashing down, and afterward it would be cool for a few hours. Then the heat came back, and curls of steam drifted up from the ground.

She watched for Kigleys while she scrubbed clothes, the smell of laundry bluing and soap all around her.

There was never a time when she was outside and not watching for Kigleys. It became exhausting.

Mrs. Stanton's cook, Nancy, came back to work, and that took a load off Bridie's shoulders. Sometimes Rose came up after school and helped mind the children. Rose also read the books on Mrs. Stanton's shelves, and she always seemed to be studying. Mostly arithmetic.

Bridie wondered if she should be studying, too. Would she be able to go to school this winter? Would Mrs. Stanton allow it? Did Bridie even want to go to school?

Rose asked Mrs. Stanton a question about something in her arithmetic book.

"Oh, goodness, it's been so long since I studied it." Mrs. Stanton picked up the book and looked at it. "The angles of the triangle have to add up to one hundred and eighty degrees. Why do you even want to know this, Rose?"

"The same reason you wanted to know it, Mrs. Stanton," said Rose.

This was talking back, and Mrs. Stanton frowned.

"I beg your pardon," said Rose, not sounding particularly sorry.

Mrs. Stanton gave her a harried look and went upstairs to see after little Gat, who was sick with the ague again.

"Why *do* you want to know it?" Bridie asked.

"Because numbers explain everything," said Rose.

"Oh," said Bridie.

"Did you know there are nearly three times as many slaves in the United States today as there were in 1800?" said Rose.

"No," said Bridie.

"It's like we're not doing anything," said Rose. "When we help people escape. It's like cutting off the head of a what-do-you-call-it."

"But it matters to the people you help," said Bridie.

"I don't think Mrs. Stanton likes me knowing things that most people don't know except her," said Rose.

Bridie worked this out. She wasn't sure if it was true or not. "Can't you ask your teacher?"

"I think . . ." Rose fiddled with the corner of a page. "I think I'm getting to the part of the book where Mr. Davis doesn't know it either."

Bridie was surprised. "You're only halfway into it!"

"Yes, but most teachers don't really know mathematics. I mean, they mostly didn't go to a fancy academy like Mrs. Stanton did." Rose was looking worried.

Bridie could see that there were a lot more pages in the book. And she knew Rose would want to learn them all.

Mrs. Stanton came downstairs. "I ought to sit up with him tonight—"

There was a loud, frantic knock at the front door.

Mrs. Stanton went to open it. A white woman burst in, disheveled and out of breath from running.

"You've got to come down to the Flats, Mrs. Stanton! Mikey is fittin' to kill his wife if she don't kill him first!"

Mrs. Stanton went. She got called on to break up fights and arguments a lot. Maybe it was because her father was a judge.

❦

On Sunday, Gat was better, and Mrs. Stanton announced that she was going to a tea party in Waterloo, the next town over. She wanted Bridie and Rose to go along to watch the children.

Mrs. Stanton wouldn't take them on the train, because a man had been killed jumping out of it just the day before. Mrs. Stanton worried that the boys would take it into their heads to jump out of the train. So she rented a horse and buggy from the livery stable.

It was hard to cram everybody into the carriage. There was Mrs. Stanton, who was driving, with Neil and Gat sitting on either side of her, and Bridie and Rose in back with four-year-old Kit.

They jounced along over roads corduroyed with logs. They bounced and flew into the air every time they hit a crooked log, and everyone but Mrs. Stanton got the giggles so hard they almost fell out of the carriage.

At last they reached Jane and Richard Hunt's house, on the outskirts of Waterloo. It was a grand brick mansion, with tall white fluted columns in front. These must be very rich people, Bridie thought. She thought so even more when they got inside—there were carpets, and sofas, and camphene lamps, and all the things that rich people had.

Mrs. Hunt came to greet them. She was carrying a very new baby, and Mrs. Stanton cooed over the baby and pulled back the blanket to look at its tiny red face.

"Isn't she the most precious thing ever!"

Bridie and Rose exchanged a glance. It looked about like a baby to them.

The blanket the baby was wrapped in was embroidered with the words

Think of the poor slave mother

when HER child is torn away

"What a little darling!" Mrs. Stanton fussed over the baby. "Does she find her anti-slavery wardrobe sufficiently supplied?"

"Yes, we were lucky to find a few yards of cotton grown by free labor. I'm so glad thee could come, Lizzie. And the children, of course—"

Mrs. Hunt looked a bit doubtful about this last item, which meant that the children were about to be sent outside. That was fine with Bridie. There were a lot of adults here and you could tell they were getting ready to talk about boring stuff.

Tiny Mrs. Mott from the Fourth of July was there, and her sister Martha Coffin Wright, and a lady named Mary Ann McClintock with her grown-up daughter Elizabeth. They all kept saying *thee* instead of *you*, which meant they were all Quakers, except Mrs. Stanton, of course.

Mrs. Mott came over and said, "Good afternoon, Phoebe."

Bridie was surprised the old lady remembered her. People mostly didn't notice Bridie, let alone remember her. She curtsied and said how-do-you-do.

To Bridie's relief, the babies were put upstairs for a nap, to be watched over by one of Mrs. Hunt's servants.

The older children were sent outside, where ten-year-old Richard pointed out that there were enough of them to play Run Sheep Run.

It was the most fun Bridie had had in forever.

Rose and Richard were the team captains. Bridie was on Rose's team. They hid behind the icehouse, and when it looked like Richard's team was about to find them, Rose yelled, "Run, sheep, run!" and they all dashed around the house and hid behind the fluted columns.

Richard sent his team after them. Rose yelled, "Run, sheep, run!" again, and they ran to the barn, with Richard's team howling in pursuit. From there they fled to the woodshed, and then down toward the creek bed, where they were finally caught.

They were all lying down on the ground, panting with exhaustion, when Mrs. Hunt's servant came out and said, "You children need to play something quieter. It's *Sunday*. Or rather First Day, I should say. Mary, come in and get some cookies for your guests."

Nine-year-old Mary grabbed Bridie by the sleeve. "Come with me!"

Bridie went. She expected they would go into the kitchen. But Mary led the way to the parlor, where the adults were all sitting around the tea table, talking earnestly.

"And when you consider that, even with the new married woman's property law, a woman still doesn't have the right to her own wages!" Mrs. Stanton was saying.

Bridie stopped cold. That was what had happened. That was how she and her mother had ended up at the poorhouse. Bridie had thought it was something that had just happened to *them*. But now the women at the table were talking about it as if it was a big problem, one that affected lots of people.

"If there's to be a convention, then I do hope it will be before Mr. Mott and I leave the area," said Mrs. Mott.

"It will have to be," said Mrs. McClintock. "People will come just to hear the famous Lucretia Mott speak, I'm sure."

Bridie looked at the tiny Mrs. Mott with renewed interest. She hadn't known she was famous.

"And, Lucretia, thee is the only one of us who can give a speech, really—" said Mrs. Wright.

"I'm sure all of us can give speeches if we set our minds to it," said Mrs. Stanton, with some asperity.

"Thee is going to write some sort of manifesto for us, Lizzie—"

Bridie and Mary just stood there and waited to be noticed. They had both been taught that children should be seen and not heard. Bridie looked at the teapot on the table, which bore the words

HEALTH TO THE SICK
HONOUR TO THE BRAVE
SUCCESS TO THE LOVER
FREEDOM TO THE SLAVE

"A declaration of some kind—" someone said.

"Do you think there's time to have an actual convention, though, with just a few days' notice?"

"More than a week—"

"If we put a notice in the paper—"

"Where should we have the convention?"

"The Wesleyan Meeting House. Thee knows they are abolitionists there and—"

"And it will be mostly abolitionists that show up, if anyone does." Mrs. Hunt turned to Mrs. Stanton.

"Could thee see about renting the building, Lizzie? And put a notice in the paper."

"I wonder if Frederick Douglass would come."

"We can ask. And Lydia Maria Child?"

"It's too far for her, but she might send a letter. . . ."

Finally someone noticed Bridie and Mary. The girls waited while the women gathered up cookies and wrapped them in a napkin. Bridie and Mary said thank you and took them outside to the others.

There were ginger snaps, and lemon jumbles, and sugar cookies, and everyone had one of each. Bridie ate hers slowly, savoring each sweet and spicy crumb, and decided she liked the lemon jumbles best.

Since they'd been told Run Sheep Run was too noisy, they played Sardines instead. Bridie was It. She hid behind the kindling box next to the back steps. Rose found her first and crawled in beside her.

"I should be studying my arithmetic," said Rose as they watched a spider crawl across the edge of the box.

"You have to have fun *some*time," said Bridie.

"But Mr. Davis keeps getting headaches, and then there's the big boys."

"Big boys?" said Bridie.

"In the winter the big boys come to school, and

they pick a fight with the teacher. The teacher has to be able to win the fight."

"What, he has to win against all of them together?" Bridie wasn't sure what this had to do with Rose.

"Yes," said Rose. "It's kind of traditional."

"Oh," said Bridie.

There were some things about America that she found very strange.

"That didn't happen when I went to school on State Street," she added.

And it certainly didn't happen at the poorhouse school. For one thing, there hadn't been any big boys.

"Yes, but the school at Locust Hill is more of a country school," said Rose. "It's a country tradition. I don't think Mr. Davis could win."

"I'm surprised anyone could win," said Bridie.

"Well, the school board generally looks for a man who has a fighting chance," said Rose. "For the winter term, anyway. If Mr. Davis leaves, then I might not get another chance to go to school."

"But if you think you're already running out of the arithmetic he knows—"

"I think he's studying at night to keep up with me."

"Can't you learn it on your own? You can read."

It was generally held that if you could read and spell, and had beautiful handwriting, you could take it from there.

"It's hard, though. And I want to be a scientist."

The spider made its way down the side of the box.

"Why?" said Bridie. She'd never, ever heard a girl say she wanted to be something before. For the first time, she wondered if *she* wanted to be something.

"I want to find out things. Mankind is finding out all sorts of new things these days about how the world works, and how the stars work, and how *we* work, just . . . everything."

"Well, *man*kind," Bridie pointed out.

"Doesn't mean I can't do it too. Did you know there's a woman studying to be a doctor right now, right over in Geneva?"

Geneva was the next town over from Waterloo. Of course Bridie knew. Everyone knew. It was in all the newspapers. People sometimes went to Geneva just to catch a glimpse of this strange woman, Elizabeth Blackwell.

"And there's a woman who found a comet—her name is Maria Mitchell. She just found it. Just last winter she published a paper about it in her father's name, but then people found out it was her."

Neil slipped into the hiding space. "I heard you talking; that's how I found you."

Bridie and Rose had scooted over to make room for him.

Bridie was thinking about what Rose had said. Imagine wanting to be something. She thought of all the things that boys could grow up to do. Boys could be doctors, and sailors, and college professors. They could be stonemasons and carpenters. They could be railroad engineers and newspaper reporters.

Supposing a girl could do any of those things. What would *she* want to do?

10

DANGER AT HOSKINS'S STORE

The next day Bridie was sent over the river to run some errands. She walked with Rose, who had just gotten out of school.

Bridie had to pick up a loaf of sugar from the store, and take a message about renting the Wesleyan Chapel to one of the church trustees, and drop off a notice to be published in the *Seneca County Courier*.

She and Rose crossed the bridge, passing a honking flock of geese. It was a hot day, and Bridie was glad she wasn't cooped up in one of the factories creaking and rattling away on the river.

A mule on the towpath flicked its ears, and a boat-man sang out, "Low bridge!" as a barge slid past beneath them.

Fall Street was crowded and dusty and smelled of too many horses. Rose said she would drop off the note about the rental with Mr. Wright, who lived near her. He was one of the trustees. The Wesleyan Chapel was the only strictly abolitionist church in town, and the only church with both colored and white trustees.

Bridie went into the newspaper office. Behind the high wooden counter sat the printing press, its iron jaws open. A boy about her own age was setting type, choosing the metal letters and sliding them into a composing stick so quickly that Bridie was amazed.

She handed Mrs. Stanton's notice to Mr. Milliken, the editor.

He looked at it. "Women's *rights* convention! Don't women have too many rights already?"

"I don't know." Bridie thought of her mother, and of what had happened at the mill and how they'd ended up in the poorhouse. "Maybe you should come to the convention and find out."

Mr. Milliken peered at the notice. "July nine-teenth and twentieth? It says, 'On the first day, the

95

meeting will be exclusively for Women, Which all are earnestly invited to attend.' Which is it?"

"Which is what?" said Bridie.

"Women, or All? Can't be both."

Mr. Milliken sounded amused, and Bridie was incensed on Mrs. Stanton's behalf. "I could take the notice somewhere else," she said.

America was swimming in newspapers. Every little town had one, or two, or five. Big cities had hundreds. Seneca Falls had at least four.

"No, no, I'm just teasing," said Mr. Milliken. "The *Courier* believes in rights. Here, Davey! Put this on page three, column two."

The boy, Davey, came up and took the notice. He was wearing a blue apron, and he was covered in ink.

Bridie felt jealous of him. Imagine working here every day, instead of pumping and hauling endless water and scrubbing things so they could be made dirty again.

Davey smiled at her. "Want to watch me set the type?"

Bridie did. Mr. Milliken lifted up a section of the counter, and Bridie went back to the machine.

"It'll go right there," said Davey, pointing to an empty square.

Just below it, Bridie saw the words !WOƆ TƧO⅃.

96

The backward lettering would come out frontward on the printed page.

The boy picked up an empty composing stick and started selecting the type, and, fascinated, Bridie watched ᴢ-'-ᴨ-ᴐ-ᴍ-o-W go into the stick.

"You can do the next word if you want," Davey offered.

Bridie did want. He handed her the composing stick.

The moment it was in her hand, it felt like it belonged there.

She held it for a moment. She felt as if she was standing on the edge of something important. It was like when she'd boarded the Canada-bound ship in Liverpool with her mother. It wasn't a scary feeling, exactly. A new world was waiting beyond the edge. She just had to jump.

Davey pointed. "You pick out the capital R from the upper case, and then the other letters from this case; it's called lower case."

She searched through the partitioned box for the Rs, found them, and put one in—"Other way, it's upside down," said Davey—and turned it around, and then went to the lower case and reached for the i, and the g . . . h . . . t . . . s.

"And now you slide it into the press."

Still with that feeling of standing on the edge of something important, she slid the letters into place, in the empty square over the !WOƆ TƧO⅃.

Davey pursed his lips and nodded. "That's how you do it. Now don't touch anything. Here."

He handed her a rag. Bridie took it and realized her hands were smeared all over with black ink.

She wiped her hands vigorously on the rag. Some of the ink came off, but it seemed her hands were going to be stained for a long time.

"It'll wear off eventually. It never does with me. . . ." Davey displayed his ink-stained hands.

Bridie didn't care whether it wore off or not. She'd put words into a printing press! Well, just one word, but it would go out into the world and people would read it and maybe that word would still be out there a hundred years from now.

The word ꙅʇɥǫiЯ. *Rights.* She'd set the type herself.

"Thank you," she said.

"No problem," said Davey.

Bridie stepped back out into the bright sunshine. The street still seemed the same as when she'd walked in—horses and wagons and people and a couple of wandering pigs—but Bridie was different. She was like Rose now: She wanted to *be* something. Specifically, she wanted to be a printer.

She didn't know how she could make that happen. But somehow she would.

Meanwhile, she had work to do. She went to Hoskins's store and asked for a sugar loaf. Mr. Hoskins went to a shelf behind the counter, where a row of cone-shaped sugar loaves stood in their blue paper wrappers. "Large or small?"

"Small, please." Even the small ones weighed several pounds.

He took one down. "Stantons' account?"

He looked through his file box, found the Stantons' card, and wrote down four shillings. Bridie signed her initials beside it, remembering to write *P* for Phoebe instead of *B* for Bridie.

As she was doing this, she glanced out the window. And she almost dropped the pencil. Dobbin the horse looked back at her, flicking his ears at flies. The Kigleys' farm wagon had just pulled up outside. Mr. Kigley was climbing out. He said something to Mrs. Kigley and then headed across the street— toward the saloon, it looked like.

Bridie watched, transfixed. She was trapped if any of them should come in here. And she couldn't leave; they were right in front of the door.

Mrs. Kigley was hauling a bundle out of the back of the wagon—oh no. She was bringing something to trade, which meant she was going to come into the store.

"Mr. Hoskins, can I go out the back door?" said Bridie hastily.

Mrs. Kigley and Lavinia were headed right for the front door of the store.

"Why?" said Mr. Hoskins.

"Because, um—" Bridie thought wildly. The Kigleys were at the door now. Through the glass panes Bridie could see a hand-shaped purple bruise on Mrs. Kigley's face. "Um, it embarrasses me to be seen carrying a sugar loaf."

"Why should it? My sugar is *not* produced with slave labor."

The front door opened. "Please!" said Bridie urgently.

Mr. Hoskins rolled his eyes. But he lifted a section of counter for Bridie to slide through, and he pointed her to a door at the back.

Bridie didn't have time to thank him—she fled.

"Who's that?" came Lavinia's voice.

"Hired girl that works for the Stantons," said Mr. Hoskins.

"What's her name?" Mrs. Kigley sounded suspicious.

"Phoebe," said Mr. Hoskins as Bridie ducked out the back door and closed it behind her.

Had Mrs. Kigley seen her? Bridie wasn't sure. She needed to get away from here, fast. She was on the steep riverbank, and she half slid, half climbed down it. The blue paper wrapping of the sugar loaf got a bit dusty.

She cut down toward the canal and crossed the catwalk by the factories in the Flats. Even with all the houses, shops, and factories on Fall Street hiding her from the Kigleys, she still felt safer taking a roundabout route. After she'd crossed the river and the canals on the factories' footbridges, she went around the sawmill and up the hill to the Stantons' house.

Mrs. Stanton was at her writing desk, with heaps of letters open before her.

"Oh, how nice, here's one from my husband."

Bridie wasn't sure if Mrs. Stanton was talking to her or not.

"He says he's becoming quite the Free Soil Party lion. Thousands of people are coming to hear his speeches. Isn't that nice? Goodness, how did you get so dirty, Phoebe?"

"From the printing press," said Bridie. She looked down at the dust on her dress, from sliding down the riverbank. "And just . . . stuff."

"Are they going to print our notice?"

"Yes, I watched them set the type myself."

"You must have watched very closely."

"They let me set one of the words!" Bridie burst out. "I want to be a printer."

There was a moment in which the words hung on the air. Saying it aloud made it seem real. Preposterous, perhaps, but real.

"Well, perhaps you'll marry one," said Mrs. Stanton. "Then you can help him in the shop and, who knows, he might leave it to you when he dies."

That sounded like an unnecessarily complicated way to go about learning a trade. "I don't want a husband," said Bridie. "I just want to be a printer."

Mrs. Stanton gave her a long, thoughtful look. Then she said, "Well, be sure you clean up before dinner."

She looked back at her husband's letter. "It's what he's doing that's going to be remembered, you know. The Free Soil Party. Imagine, a whole new political party, just to keep slavery from spreading to the new territories. No one will remember *our* little convention. But one must start somewhere."

She shuffled through her pile of letters. "Frederick Douglass and Amy Post are both coming down from Rochester on the train, and we'll have my sister and the Motts and . . . I wonder if any of them can stay at the American Hotel. . . . Oh dear. Phoebe, I'm afraid you'll have to give up your room."

"They're all staying *here?*" said Bridie, surprised.

"Most likely. Let me see—I'll move the boys in with me, and then if we put you at the top of the stairs, we can put Mrs. Mott and her sister in the boys' room, and Frederick Douglass and Mr. Mott—"

There was a sudden crack of thunder. Mrs. Stanton jumped; she did *not* like loud noises.

"The laundry's outside!" said Bridie.

She and Mrs. Stanton ran outside. The sky was a menacing dark gray. Hurriedly they gathered clothes from the clothesline and bushes, while the thunder rolled and lightning flashed. A pair of drawers escaped, and Bridie had to chase them across the yard before she caught them.

Laden with still-damp clothes, Bridie and Mrs. Stanton ran inside just as the first big raindrops came splatting down.

⚜

For the next few days, Bridie and Rose were busy getting the house ready for all the visitors. Mrs. Stanton helped sometimes, but mostly she spent her time writing her declaration for the convention. Bridie saw her working on it late into the night, by the light of the camphene lamp, muttering to herself, "When in the course of human events . . ."

Rose was terribly excited about Frederick Douglass.

Bridie didn't understand why. "Who is he?"

"A colored man who runs a *newspaper*," said Rose.

Bridie must have looked unimpressed. Lots of men ran newspapers. Now, if a woman ran a newspaper, that would be news.

"And he wrote a book," said Rose. "He escaped from slavery and wrote a book about it, which a whole lot of people have read, including me. And he makes speeches against slavery; he travels all over to do it, even to England and Ireland."

Ireland.

"Like Mrs. Stanton's husband, then," said Bridie.

"Only a lot more so." Rose gave up on trying to explain.

"Why's he coming to a women's rights meeting, then?" said Bridie.

"Because he's for women's rights. Just about everyone who's coming is an abolitionist," said Rose. "It's human rights."

There was that phrase again. *Human rights.* Bridie thought about everything that had happened in Ireland, and how the people had starved while the grain they grew was taken away from them and the houses they lived in were pulled down by the landlords.

Then she thought about Mr. Douglass's newspaper. He must have a printing press.

11

DISTINGUISHED VISITORS

Bridie and Rose were helping Nancy, the cook, make a fricassee of chicken. The day was much too hot for cooking, but there had to be something for dinner, especially with guests expected. At least they could do some of the work outside. The girls were out on the back stoop, plucking chickens, when they heard the first guests arrive.

There was a distant roll of thunder.

"I hope a storm's not going to come and ruin Mrs. Stanton's convention," said Rose.

"Well, it's inside. In the Wesleyan Chapel."

"Yes, but people have to get there. They won't come if it rains. Or not as many people."

The girls looked to the north, where they could see dark storm clouds passing on the horizon.

"It must be raining on the Erie Canal," said Rose.

"Amy! Frederick!" Mrs. Stanton's voice came through the screen door. "How delightful that you could both come. Why, Amy, what is this?"

"A small gift made by the Rochester Ladies' Anti-Slavery Society and Sewing Circle," said a woman's voice.

"How lovely, what fine stitching. I'll take it through to the kitchen—and Frederick, this is your new newspaper?"

"The *North Star*. Hot off the press. Possibly still a bit wet behind the ears." The man had a deep, rolling voice and a somewhat sardonic tone.

"There can't be many editors of color in the country," said Mrs. Stanton.

"Four, as it happens," said the man. "Now that I may count myself among that number."

"I like the masthead. 'Right is of no sex—Truth is of no color. . . .' Did you have any trouble on the trip down?"

"The usual difficulty," said the man. "The train conductor labored under the misapprehension that, despite having purchased a ticket as a human, I would prefer to ride in the baggage car. I disabused him of the notion."

"He hadn't met Frederick before," said the woman. "Now he has."

Bridie and Rose had come into the too-hot kitchen to see the new arrivals, bringing a dead chicken with them.

Mrs. Stanton came in holding a pot holder and handed it to Bridie, who took it with her unchickened hand. Embroidered on the pot holder were a man and woman dancing and the words

Any Holder but a Slaveholder

Rose, meanwhile, had gone to the doorway and was staring into the parlor at the visitors. Bridie went and joined her. She saw a tall, impeccably dressed colored man with sharp eyes that missed nothing, and an elderly white lady with a formidable nose and a mouth that looked ready to laugh.

"These are Phoebe and Rose, who are a great help to me," said Mrs. Stanton. "Phoebe, Rose, meet Mrs. Post and Mr. Douglass."

Both girls curtsied, Bridie with difficulty because she was still holding the pot holder and the dead chicken.

Bridie felt a rush of pride at being called helpful in front of these clearly important people from

Rochester. As for Rose, she was staring at Mr. Douglass and looking positively awestruck.

"Girls, why don't you show—" Mrs. Stanton glanced at the dead chicken. "Rose, show Mr. Douglass and Mrs. Post to their rooms, please."

Rose went off to lead the way upstairs, and Bridie went back to plucking the chicken while the cook chopped vegetables. The kitchen filled with a grand smell of frying onions.

❧

Rose turned left at the top of the stairs. It was too hot upstairs, even with the windows open. You could smell the floorboards baking.

"Mrs. Post, you're in here," said Rose, "and there will be some other ladies coming tomorrow, um, and they'll be in here with you and, um, I guess you probably want some water for washing which is in the well."

This sounded dumb to Rose, and she hastily added, "And I'll get it for you," and wished that Mr. Davis had let her recite more often in school so that she'd be better prepared to speak on important occasions.

"That's fine, dear; I can get it," said Mrs. Post.

"All right, um, good." Rose led Mr. Douglass back across the landing. Now she was really nervous. Mr. Douglass was the most famous colored man in America; quite possibly the most famous colored man in the world.

She knew he had been enslaved in Maryland, and that he had escaped by getting on a train and riding north to New York City, where he'd gotten married and changed his name twice to avoid pursuit. And he was a famous speaker against slavery, who traveled all over the place, and people paid money to hear him— *white* people paid money to hear a *colored* man.

"Um, so, um, this is your, um, room," said Rose to the famous speaker.

Mr. Douglass sat down on one of the beds.

"And, um, Mr. Mott will be in it with you tomorrow if he gets over what's ailing him and, um, water," said Rose.

She was really mangling this.

Mr. Douglass smiled. "Rose: that's almost like my daughter's name. How old are you, Rose?"

"Eleven, sir."

"My Rosetta is nine. And do you go to school?"

"Yes, sir. For as long as I can."

"And your parents, they live here in Seneca Falls? What does your father do?"

"My mother's dead and my father's on a whaling ship." Rose found herself talking more easily now. Mr. Douglass was only human, after all, especially now that he was sitting down. "That is, he was on a whaling ship, but now I don't know, because I haven't heard from him in a long time."

Mr. Douglass winced sympathetically. He did not need any explanation of what that meant. "What is his name?"

"David Wilson."

Mr. Douglass took a small notebook and a pencil out of his pocket and jotted something down. "I shall make inquiries. I know people in New Bedford and Nantucket, where the whaling ships dock."

He put the notebook and pencil away, and Rose suddenly had the impression that he'd made just that same motion many times, with the same not-too-hopeful expression on his face each time.

And Rose didn't *want* to hope. She'd hoped when her mother was sick, and it hadn't helped. But she found now that she couldn't help it.

"Thank you, sir," she said.

"And so you live with Mrs. Stanton?"

"No, sir. I board with Mr. Ferris Moody over on State Street, and I make a living doing deliveries and errands for the factories," said Rose. "And a bit of extra work now and then, like helping Mrs. Stanton."

"And with all of that, you still manage your schooling? A veritable wonder!"

"I'm a little bit in ar . . ." Rose searched for the right word. "Arr . . . behind with my rent, but Mr. Moody will wait till the school term's over."

"Arrears?" said Mr. Douglass. "Hmm. We'll see what we can do about that."

Rose felt shy; she hadn't been asking for help and she certainly hadn't meant to beg. "I manage, sir. Do you think my father's been kidnapped and sold?"

She blurted it out all at once and then stood twisting her hands and waiting for him to answer.

"I don't know, Rose." He said it like he did know. "I know that my friend Mrs. Sojourner Truth hasn't heard from her sailor son in years, and she has similar concerns. However, while there is life there is, of course, the usual."

"Hope," said Rose.

"Precisely so. And if all else fails, you know, you can simply come and move in with the Douglasses. Everyone else does, and my wife is quite accustomed to it. There are plenty of schools in Rochester."

Rose stared.

"The accommodations are not quite as commodious as this," he added, looking around Mrs. Stanton's spare room. "Right now we have ten fugitives sleeping on a carpet in the attic, until we can raise money to buy them boat tickets to Canada. But we all cram in somehow."

"I help out with the Underground Railroad sometimes," said Rose proudly.

"Do you! Excellent. And yet how I wish that our white friends did not trumpet the Railroad's existence. Far better that the slaveholders should wonder how their so-called property keeps mysteriously disappearing northward."

Rose felt somewhat rebuked.

"Tell me of your schooling. Does your teacher treat you just the same as the white students?" Mr. Douglass looked concerned, and Rose remembered his daughter Rosetta and thought he might be thinking about her.

"Not exactly. He never lets me recite."

"And does he expound some reason for this?"

"Parents might complain."

Mr. Douglass sighed. "Here in York State, so much more is expected of us. Everything we do is taken as a sign of how much colored people can or cannot do. But if we succeed too much, we are thought to be taking something from our white countrymen."

"But Mr. Davis just ignores me!"

"No doubt he talks about you more than his other students. He probably discusses your successes and failures with his friends as a sign of what the colored race can and cannot accomplish."

Rose found this thought extremely depressing. She was just *Rose*; she didn't want to be a sign of anything.

She told Mr. Douglass about the arithmetic.

"What! Girls not learn arithmetic! But my wife, Anna, excels at it, although she cannot even read. She is the banker of the family. She counts, adds, multiplies, and most frequently, in the nature of things, is obliged to subtract."

Rose wished Mr. Douglass would tell Mr. Davis this.

"Not only that. I know of a young colored lady, also named Davis, who is a special student in mathematics at an academy in Massachusetts, *and* she intends to become a physician."

Rose was astonished at this, and felt suddenly hopeful. "There's a lady over in Geneva studying to be a doctor, but she's white."

"And just in the nick of time, both of them," said Mr. Douglass. "For I fear our country is headed to war."

Rose had not heard this before. "With who?

Whom," she corrected herself. Mr. Douglass was clearly the sort of person to notice whether you *who*ed when you should have *whom*ed.

"With ourselves, over slavery. I used to think otherwise, but I recently spoke to a wool merchant in Massachusetts named John Brown, and he convinced me that the only way forward is through a sea of blood. America will not give up slavery without a fight."

This was overwhelming and big. Rose didn't know what she wanted to happen. A sea of blood sounded really bad. Then again, she thought of some of the fugitives that she'd helped, the ones who'd come through on the Underground Railroad. She thought of some of the stories they'd told. A sea of blood didn't sound like *enough*.

"I'll get you some water," said Rose.

She went downstairs, her head full of all the large ideas that Mr. Douglass had filled it with.

And he might be able to find her father. He hadn't sounded very confident. But he knew people he could ask.

She tried not to hope. She needed to help get dinner.

12

JULY 19

In the morning the sky was bright and clear. The storms had passed by to the north, and left Seneca Falls undrenched. There was a great fuss of getting ready for the first day of the first-ever women's rights convention. There were books and papers to find, and sandwiches to be made and packed.

Mrs. Stanton's sister Harriet Cady Eaton had arrived late the night before with her son, Daniel, who was about Bridie's age.

Since men weren't supposed to come to the first day of the convention, Frederick Douglass had gone off to visit friends and try to sell subscriptions to his newspaper. Mrs. Stanton had decreed that Daniel, at eleven, didn't count as a man, and that he should come and so should Bridie, to hear the improving speeches and to understand the issues of the day.

Rose was at school. Mrs. Post had gone out early to visit an old friend. Mrs. Stanton, Mrs. Eaton, Daniel, and Bridie set out together. Everyone was laden with books and picnic baskets.

Daniel and Bridie followed behind, while the adults walked along and talked.

"What if no one comes?" said Mrs. Stanton.

"Someone's bound to," said Mrs. Eaton. "The notice was in all the papers."

"I only sent it to the *Courier*."

"But all the other papers picked it up. All the way to Rochester."

Bridie was impressed. That message she'd carried, the one that Davey had set in type (except for the word *Rights*, which was Bridie's) had gone out for miles and miles, starting from Seneca Falls.

"Well, someone is bound to show up, I suppose," said Mrs. Stanton. "And what if it's a crowd? I'll have to speak in front of all of them. I don't know if I can do it."

"You're worried that no one will show up and

you're worried that everyone will show up," said Mrs. Eaton, sounding amused.

"I'm as nervous as a long-tailed cat in a room full of rocking chairs," Mrs. Stanton admitted.

They crossed the bridge and walked up the steep slope. As soon as they turned onto Fall Street, they saw the crowd.

From here, they could mostly see wide skirts and top hats.

Top hats?

"The men weren't supposed to come today! It was in the notice! Men were only invited for the second day."

"Calm down, Lizzie," said Mrs. Eaton. "I'm sure if we—"

"Remember what happened in Philadelphia!"

"This is Seneca Falls," said Mrs. Eaton.

"What happened in Philadelphia?" Bridie asked Daniel. He seemed like a bookish sort of boy who might know.

"A women's anti-slavery society met, and some men came and attacked them and burned down the hall," said Daniel.

"But they weren't men in top hats, I'm sure," said his mother, giving him a quelling glance.

They had reached the Wesleyan Chapel. Everyone was standing around, fanning themselves and looking far too warm in their wool and linen clothes—they must all be anti-slavery folks, Bridie thought, and was grateful for her cotton poorhouse dress.

Still, she'd never thought before about the cotton being grown by slaves.

"The door's locked," said a man.

There were a lot of men. Dozens. And even more women. Two hundred? More? They filled the sidewalk and spilled over into the street.

Mrs. Mott came hurrying down State Street from the train station. "Does thee not have the key, Lizzie?"

Mrs. Stanton shook her head.

"I can climb in the window," said Daniel. "I found one that's unlocked."

"Gentlemen," said Mrs. Mott, her voice ringing out through the crowd, "please be mindful of the rules of the convention. Since you are here, we will be pleased to admit you—"

"Admit the gentlemen? To a meeting where only ladies will speak? Unheard of!"

"—but we ask that you please remain silent until tomorrow's meeting."

"They'll never do that," a woman muttered.

A man beside her looked affronted.

Bridie and Daniel managed to work the unlocked window upward with their fingernails.

"Hoist me up," said Daniel.

Bridie wanted to climb in, but she couldn't in her dress and stockings, not in front of all these people. So she made a step with her hands. Daniel put one foot into it and shoved off. Just for a second he was very heavy, and Bridie winced at the gritty shoe leather biting into her palms. Then he was through the window.

A moment later he had the door unbarred, and people were pouring into the church. It was a large, plain building, all one room, with whitewashed walls, a balcony around three sides, and a pulpit at the front. The crowd filled the rows of wooden pews.

"Women's rights indeed," said one of the men, stowing his top hat under the pew. "You see how women take up twice as much room as men?"

"That's because of these ridiculous petticoats on top of petticoats on top of more petticoats," said the woman beside him, sounding annoyed. "We all look like dinner bells! If we could wear sensible clothes . . ."

She unfolded a fan and began fanning herself.

The pews were so crowded that people were beginning to go up to the balcony.

"A bit warm in here, isn't it?"

"Someone open the windows."

People were fluttering fans and newspapers and anything they could find that would make a breeze.

Bridie went up to the balcony to help open windows. It was tarnation hot up here. And yet there were women and a few men filing into the pews, looking earnest. They must really want to be here.

Or else they were here to cause trouble. Bridie thought of what Daniel had said about Philadelphia.

Speaking of trouble . . . Bridie put her head out an open window and looked up and down the street for Kigleys. No Kigleys in sight.

When she came back downstairs, Mrs. Stanton, Mrs. Mott, and the McClintock ladies had gathered at the front by the podium. Mrs. Stanton was digging through her papers.

"Here's my speech. I suppose I'd better begin by making it."

She looked nervous. The other women encouraged her.

"Thee will do fine, Lizzie."

"Don't worry."

"Remember thy temperance speech, thee did that—"

"What if this whole idea is ridiculous?" Mrs. Stanton said.

"Thee sees this crowd here, they don't think it's ridiculous."

"They're here to hear you, Lucretia. I can't find it!" Mrs. Stanton pawed frantically at her papers.

"Thy speech? It's right there."

"No, no, the Declaration of Sentiments! It's gone! Did any of you bring a copy?"

The other women looked at each other.

"Thee was going to write in the changes we suggested, and make a fair copy, Lizzie."

"I did that! It's not here!"

"Perhaps thee left it home."

"Oh!" Mrs. Stanton brightened. "Yes, I must have. I'm as nervous as a mule on an icy towpath." She looked around and saw Bridie. "Run home and get it for me, please, Phoebe. It's on my desk and says 'Declaration of Sentiments' at the top. And hurry. I'll need it by the time Mrs. Mott finishes her speech."

"Yes, ma'am." Bridie went, making her way through the church with all the people talking to each other and fanning themselves.

Bridie knew she had to hurry. It was a long way back to Mrs. Stanton's house. Still, she had time. She figured Mrs. Stanton's opening speech would be long. And then Mrs. Mott would speak; she was a famous speaker and the crowd would be eager to hear her. Most people considered long speeches prime entertainment.

Bridie stepped out the church door . . . and ran smack into the Kigleys.

13

THE DECLARATION OF SENTIMENTS

Bridie crashed right into Mrs. Kigley and Lavinia.

They hardly seemed to notice Bridie. They pushed right past her and hurried on up Fall Street.

Mr. Kigley wasn't with them. Bridie noticed that Mrs. Kigley still had that hand-shaped mark on her face, and Lavinia had welts on her arms, as if she'd clawed through a patch of nettles. Or been hit by a belt.

Bridie stood staring after them. Lavinia turned and looked back at her, and then pulled her mother's sleeve and said something.

Well. Bridie needed to hurry to get Mrs. Stanton's Declaration of Sentiments. She dodged across the street, between horses and wagons, narrowly missed stepping in a pile of manure, and trotted down toward the bridge.

She wasn't going to worry about the Kigleys. So what if they thought Bridie belonged to them? Mrs. Stanton, who had read all those law books she had in her house, said that Bridie did *not* belong to them.

She crossed the bridge, gazing down at the islands covered with houses and factories. The factory where her mother had worked was a tall stone reminder on the opposite shore.

A duck pecked its way along the shore, followed by a bobbing row of yellow-and-black ducklings.

Bridie didn't know how long Mrs. Mott would speak—an hour probably, but she'd better not count on it. She speeded up.

On the other side of the river, Bridie turned left onto Bayard Street. Something made her look back, and she saw Mrs. Kigley and Lavinia standing on the bridge, watching her.

Bridie didn't like this at all. But she was tired of living in fear of Kigleys. She walked on.

When she reached the house, Nancy was in the kitchen making dinner, and Kit and Gat were outside crawling among the cabbages in the garden, pretending they were in a forest.

Bridie found the papers on the desk and started back down Locust Hill. She'd probably taken too long already. As she hurried along Bayard Street, she thought she saw the Kigleys standing in the doorway of a dry-goods store. But she ignored them and took a shortcut up Seneca Street toward the factory catwalks.

As she walked, she read the Declaration. It was hard to make out the words. Schools nowadays taught swooping, graceful, beautiful penmanship, but Mrs. Stanton had evidently not gone to that kind of school. Her handwriting was loose and urgent and hard to decipher, even in the bright sunlight.

Bridie figured out that the Declaration included a list of rights that women should have but didn't. And then, written in the margin, where it would have looked like an afterthought if it hadn't been in such strong, stern letters, was this:

Resolved, that it is the duty of the women of this country to secure to themselves their sacred right to the elective franchise.

Bridie couldn't figure out what this meant. But it looked like it had been added last. She wondered if it might have something to do with how nervous Mrs. Stanton had been this morning.

When Bridie got back to the church, Lucretia Mott was speaking. People had stopped fanning themselves and were leaning forward eagerly. Tiny Mrs. Mott had a strong voice and spoke in rolling, ringing tones that filled the hall up to the rafters.

Bridie hurried to the front and handed the Declaration of Sentiments to Mrs. Stanton.

"Thank you, Phoebe," said Mrs. Stanton. "Just in time. I think Lucretia's train of thought is approaching the station."

It occurred to Bridie that now that she'd decided not to hide from the Kigleys anymore, she didn't need to be called Phoebe.

But it would be awkward to explain this, especially right now with Mrs. Stanton already heading toward the podium. Besides, it was Rose's mother's name, and Bridie knew it was an honor to have been given it and it ought not to be lightly tossed aside. Besides-besides, Bridie kind of liked it.

Mrs. Mott finished speaking. Applause rippled, then rolled across the room.

A wooden apple crate had been set behind the

pulpit for Mrs. Mott to stand on, Bridie saw. Mrs. Mott got down from it. Her sister Mrs. Wright came up and said, "Thee spoke well, Lucretia."

Mrs. Stanton mounted the apple crate, put the papers Bridie had brought in front of her, took a deep breath, and began to read her Declaration of Sentiments.

" 'When, in the course of human events, it becomes necessary for one portion of the family of man to assume among the people of the earth a position different from that which they have hitherto occupied . . .' "

Bridie went and stood against the wall to listen; there were no empty seats.

She knew *family of man* meant everybody, whether they were men or not. This had always seemed strange to her, and it was especially confusing when you knew that Mrs. Stanton was talking about women. Bridie looked at the people in the long rows. They were leaning forward just as they had for Mrs. Mott. They weren't just here to hear a famous anti-slavery speaker. They were here for this, too.

" 'The history of mankind is a history of repeated injuries and usurpations on the part of man toward woman, having in direct object the establishment of an absolute tyranny over her. To prove this, let facts be submitted to a candid world,'" said Mrs. Stanton, her voice ringing in the big room.

Several of the men in the audience looked uncomfortable, but that could have been the heat.

"'He has not ever permitted her to exercise her right to the elective franchise!'"

Everyone started talking at once. To Bridie's relief, a lot of people were saying, "What's that mean?"

"Vote," said a man near Bridie. "It means vote."

"What! Women, vote? This is ridiculous!"

A few people got up and walked out, the door slicing a beam of sunlight across the floor as they left.

Bridie slid into one of the newly vacant seats. Everyone was talking, louder and louder.

Mrs. Stanton turned to Mrs. Mott, who said something to her that Bridie couldn't hear.

"If you'll kindly wait," said Mrs. Stanton, shouting to be heard over the hubbub, "we'll have a discussion of each of these points *after* the reading."

People quieted down, and Mrs. Stanton went back to reading. "'He has taken from her all right in property, even to the wages she earns.'"

"This is all a bit hard on men, what?" said a man near Bridie.

Someone shushed him. Bridie didn't hear what Mrs. Stanton said next. She was too busy thinking about what had just been said, right here in this church in front of hundreds of people.

Even to the wages she earns.

If that hadn't been true, if that weren't the law, Bridie's mother might have still been alive.

⚜

There was a break for refreshments, and everyone headed outside. A woman was selling lemonade from a cart.

All the adults were standing around talking, filling the wooden sidewalk, forcing passersby to step, scowling, into the dusty street. Bridie stood in line to buy lemonade. It cost five cents, and Bridie had money, because she'd been paid. Money of her own, that she'd earned by working and had been allowed to keep. This had never happened to her before.

Rose appeared beside her. "What's going on?"

"The convention." Bridie gestured. "How come you're not in school?"

"Mr. Davis sent us all home because he had the headache." Rose looked worried about this.

They were at the head of the line. "Two lemonades, please," said Bridie, proud to be able to treat her friend. You could do that sort of thing when you had a job.

Provided you were allowed to keep what you earned, that is.

The bucket of lemonade had a big chunk of ice floating in it, melting fast in the afternoon sun. The woman plunged a dipper in and filled two tin cups. "Ten cents."

Now came the confusing part. Bridie handed over an English shilling. The woman counted out Bridie's change in pennies, some English, some American, and one that Bridie didn't know where it was from. Rose watched carefully and gave a slight nod; there had been no funny business.

You had to know a lot of arithmetic to work out the hodgepodge of coins, and yet most people hardly learned any.

Beads of condensation formed on the outside of the tin cups. The girls wrapped their hands around the cool metal and went around to the side of the building. They squeezed into a narrow strip of shade and sat down.

Mrs. Stanton's nephew, Daniel, came and found them and gave them ham sandwiches, and then he went away again.

The ham sandwiches were exactly salty enough, and the cool lemonade was just the right amount of sweet and sour.

Bridie told Rose about seeing the Kigleys and about them seeing her.

"Did they say anything?" asked Rose.

"No, but I think they followed me."

"Maybe they want help."

"Help?" Bridie looked at her to see if she was joking. "From me? Mrs. Kigley and Lavinia?"

Rose, the Underground Railroad agent, shrugged. "They might need help."

"There's no way that . . ." Bridie thought of the bruises on Mrs. Kigley's face, and the welts on Lavinia's arms.

Well, it wasn't her problem.

"I hope Mr. Davis's headaches don't make the school board get rid of him," said Rose.

Bridie hadn't thought Rose was especially fond of Mr. Davis. "You said they're probably going to get a new teacher anyway, right? One that can fight the big boys."

"The new one might not let me in the school. Or might not let me study arithmetic."

"Oh." Bridie didn't know what to say to this.

She picked up Rose's arithmetic book and read a problem from it aloud. " 'Adonibizek said, "Threescore and ten kings, having their thumbs and their great toes cut off, gather their meat under my table." How many thumbs and toes did Adonibizek cut off?' "

"Two hundred and eighty," said Rose. "Read the one about baking a dead body to remove nine-tenths of its weight."

"Ugh. No thanks." Bridie wrinkled her nose; arithmetic was disgusting. She was glad to have escaped it. Even boys didn't start studying it till they were ten or so, and Bridie hadn't had much time for school since then.

They got up to take their empty cups back to the lemonade stand. There was still a crowd of people from the convention milling around.

"What I'm hoping to prove with my experiments," one of the ladies was saying, "is that different gases will cause the sun's rays to behave differently."

The woman she was talking to wore a somewhat glazed expression. "Well, I'm not quite sure what you mean, Mrs. Foote. . . ."

"I mean that human activity could affect the earth's atmosphere. Cause the earth to warm up or cool down. If only I had access to a laboratory, and could correspond with scientific colleagues, like a man . . ."

"How fascinating," said her friend politely.

Bridie noticed that Rose really did looked fascinated. This was *science*.

But science wasn't for women. Surely Rose had just heard Mrs. Foote explain that.

14

AN UNPLEASANT SURPRISE IN THE WASHHOUSE

The convention reconvened, but Rose went home to study, and Bridie went home to help make dinner. With so many people staying in the house, there was a lot to do. Usually they just had one dish for dinner—it was less work—but of course with guests, Mrs. Stanton wanted to do things up brown, with beef à la mode and vegetables and corn pudding and gooseberry custard and all sorts of things.

There were a lot of dishes that got used in the cooking and had to be washed so they could be used in the cooking some more.

So Bridie went out to the pump, again and again, to fill buckets with water and carry them inside. In the end she decided it would be less work to haul a washtub close to the pump and bring the dishes outside.

She went into the washhouse to get a tub.

The washhouse was dark and stuffy, and smelled of soap and dirt. An oaken tub hung on the wall, just visible in the gloom. The thing was heavy, and getting it down from its hook was a struggle.

As she tried to work it free, she heard something stirring behind her. Probably a woodchuck. They had a burrow under the washhouse.

Something touched her shoulder.

Bridie jumped a mile. She spun around. Lavinia Kigley stood there, just visible in the darkness.

"I'm not coming back, so you can forget that," said Bridie. "I have rights."

"No one's asking you to," said Lavinia. "We've left."

She didn't sound as haughty and, well, snotty as she used to sound back on the farm. She was talking to Bridie like an equal. It was rather discombobu-lating.

"What, you've moved to town?" Bridie didn't care; if the Kigleys had left their farm and moved into Seneca Falls, they still didn't have any right to Bridie and she still refused to be afraid.

"No, I mean Mother and I have left."

"Help me get this thing down," said Bridie.

Lavinia reached up, and together they managed to wrestle the heavy tub from the wall without dropping it on their toes.

"We had to leave. We thought he was going to kill us."

Bridie remembered the wild, animal look that got into Mr. Kigley's eyes sometimes. "That's why I left too," she said.

Not confiding. Just letting Lavinia know this wasn't Bridie's problem. After all, he wasn't *her* father.

"And don't think I've forgotten all those times you blamed stuff on me," Bridie added.

"I had to! I didn't want to get killed!"

"And you wanted me to get killed instead?"

"Well, I mean, you're just a girl from the poorhouse—"

Bridie raised her hand to hit Lavinia. It had been building up in her.

But Lavinia cringed and cowered, and Bridie instantly felt like a beast. She lowered her hand.

"Look," said Bridie, "you need to go to the

poorhouse if you haven't got anywhere else to go. They'll take you in."

"People like us don't go to the poorhouse! It's for colored people and foreigners and idiots!"

Bridie gritted her teeth. She was *not* going to hit Lavinia.

"And it's the first place my father will come looking for us," Lavinia added, "and they'll give us right back to him."

That was true. Bridie had seen it happen. After all, the poorhouse was always glad to reduce its numbers, and everyone knew that you couldn't interfere between man and wife. *Everyone* knew it. You heard it in church at every wedding.

If Mr. Kigley actually did kill his wife and daughter, *then* the law would take an interest.

Mrs. Kigley and Lavinia were in exactly the same fix Bridie had been in at their house, except that, unlike her, they didn't have rights.

"Then go somewhere else," said Bridie.

"We don't have anywhere else."

"Well, what do you expect me to do about it?"

"Let us hide here."

"In the washhouse?"

"Yes. Well, Mama's in the woodshed."

"It's not my washhouse. Or woodshed. It's Mrs. Stanton's."

This was one of the strange things about Mrs. Stanton, Bridie had learned: Her house really was her house, and not her husband's. She owned it.

"Well, everyone knows Mrs. Stanton's good at talking to men that aren't treating their families right."

Bridie thought again about that killer look in Mr. Kigley's eyes. Was Mrs. Stanton any match for that look? Should she have to be?

"Phoebe! Dishes!" came Nancy's voice from the kitchen door.

"I'll think about it," Bridie told Lavinia. She dragged the washtub out to the pump.

⚜

Bridie and Nancy and Rose, who had been hired for the evening, ate first. Then they waited on table during dinner. Bridie carried out a big dish of buttered parsnips, and Rose brought in the corn pudding, and Nancy, with a flourish, brought in the beef à la mode.

Everyone at the table bowed their heads, and Mrs. Stanton intoned, "Make us thankful for all the blessings of this life and make us ever mindful of the patient hands that often in weariness spread our tables and prepare our daily food."

Part of Mrs. Stanton's strangeness was that she had very firm ideas about who ought to be thanked for dinner.

"And are men to be permitted at your speech tonight, Lucretia?" asked Frederick Douglass as he passed the parsnips.

"They were there today!" said Daniel Eaton.

"Children are to be seen and not heard, Daniel," his mother murmured.

"As are men, and about time, no doubt. Had I known we were to be admitted, I would have gone," said Mr. Douglass.

The parsnips were all gone. Bridie went out to the kitchen to get more from the pot.

"My speech tonight will be about reform in general," Mrs. Mott was saying when she came back. "Anti-slavery, women's rights, the care of the poor, and of course famine relief in Ireland."

Most of the time Ireland stayed in a tightly closed box in Bridie's brain. But at Mrs. Mott's words it leapt out, dancing like death, and stood stark and starving in the middle of the laden table.

"I shall certainly look forward to hearing it," said Mr. Douglass.

Bridie didn't realize she was frozen in place. She saw the dark green potato leaves poking through the soil on her family's plot in Ireland. Filled every inch of the family plot, right up to the cottage door. They were bigger and greener than ever, in that year of 1845. It had looked like a good crop.

Then the rains began.

She remembered the strong plants suddenly getting dark spots, and then withering and dying overnight.

The grain harvest on the estate survived. But the grain was for the English landlord. It was not for tenants like Bridie's family.

She remembered the wagons that hauled away the grain harvest to be shipped to England, while all over Ireland, potato plants died and potatoes rotted. She remembered throwing rocks at the wagons with her brothers, Michael and Seamus.

Michael was a year older than Bridie, and good at school. Everyone said he might be a teacher himself someday. And Seamus was two years younger, and not much good at school at all, but clever with his hands. He could make things; baskets and such.

But by then, by the time they watched the wagons, she and her brothers were getting weaker. Soon they couldn't throw rocks anymore, but could only stand and stare as the wagons rolled and creaked down the dirt lane, passing other cottages of staring, starving people. Why was the grain going to England?

To pay the landlords. And when the potato crop failed again the next year, and the year after that, and people were too weak to grow grain, the landlords didn't get paid. So the landlords sent men to pull the tenants' cottages down. And then Bridie's father had gone out to break rocks for the road, to earn relief money. One day he had lifted his hammer to swing and had fallen down in the dust. And he hadn't gotten up again.

And then her brothers . . .

Bridie felt Rose take her by the arm and lead her out to the kitchen.

Bridie blinked. It was hot in the kitchen, and it smelled of beef à la mode, and Ireland was a long way away.

Rose handed Bridie a tin cup of water and Bridie gulped it down, suddenly realizing she was very thirsty.

"It's like you try to keep it locked up all the time, and then when it comes bursting out it's big enough to swallow you?" said Rose.

"Yes," said Bridie, glad she didn't have to explain. "I know how that is."

They gathered up the dishes that were ready to

be cleaned. Ireland was a long way away, and there was work to be done.

"I put a washtub out by the pump to save hauling water," said Bridie. "Oh, there's something I should tell you."

Rose listened to her explanation about Mrs. Kigley and Lavinia. "Are they well hidden?"

"I don't know. I mean, it's not the Underground Railroad, Rose."

Rose wasn't having any. "The first thing is, are they well hidden. The second thing is, do they have food, water, and conveniences."

"Well, there's conveniences out in the yard," said Bridie. "Do you think we should tell Mrs. Stanton?"

They both looked toward the dining room. Laughter and conversation filtered through the closed door.

"She's busy with her guests and her convention and everything," said Rose.

"We'll wait till after it's over and then tell her," said Bridie.

"If they haven't gone away by then," said Rose.

Bridie nodded; it was what she'd been thinking too.

"But we do have to feed them," said Rose.

Bridie opened her mouth to say that the Kigleys were horrible people who didn't deserve feeding. Then she shut it again. When you'd watched people starve all around you, when you'd been starving yourself, well, then you couldn't let other people go hungry. Besides, eating was probably a human right.

Nonetheless, after they'd brought the food in from the dining room, Bridie took a certain satisfaction in selecting the least appealing bits to take out to the Kigleys.

⚜

Taking care of the Kigleys turned out to be an infernal nuisance. They had to be fed, and water had to be pumped for them. They could have pumped at night, under cover of darkness, but when Bridie mentioned this, Mrs. Kigley sniffed and said someone would hear the pump handle creaking.

"So what if they do?" said Bridie, when she took them some bread for breakfast. "It's not the Underground Railroad."

"How dare you compare us to colored people!" said Mrs. Kigley.

"I wouldn't. All the ones I know are nicer than you," said Bridie.

"The Underground Railroad is a travesty," said Mrs. Kigley. "People ought to stay in the positions to which Providence has assigned them, and not run away."

"Except you," said Bridie.

They glared at each other for a moment. Then Mrs. Kigley looked away.

"This bread is stale," she said.

"But better than nothing," said Bridie meaningly.

"Did you tell Mrs. Stanton about us yet?" said Lavinia.

"She's busy," said Bridie.

"You mean she won't help us?"

"I mean I didn't tell her." At the desperate look in Lavinia's eyes, Bridie relented and added, "I'll tell her when all these people leave. If you're still here."

"We have nowhere else to go," said Mrs. Kigley, as if that was somehow Bridie's fault.

15

JULY 20

Lucretia Mott's husband, Mr. Mott, was to be chairman of the meeting on the second day, because men were going to be allowed to participate. Everyone agreed that having a woman in charge of a meeting where men spoke would be too shocking.

"I'm not saying it couldn't happen someday," said one of the women. "But right now it would be too much, too fast."

"Indeed. We want people's attention on the Declaration of Sentiments, not on who is chairing the meeting."

Bridie had her work to do around the house, but

late in the morning she was sent to carry some sandwiches and cakes to Mrs. Stanton and her guests, down at the Wesleyan Chapel.

It was another hot day. Bridie walked along the catwalk by the canal lock. The lock was closed, and filling slowly with water, while a long, covered canal boat waited patiently between the two sets of water doors.

She hoped Mrs. Kigley and Lavinia would be gone by dinnertime. Surely there were other places they could go. It wasn't Bridie's job to help them. She didn't owe them a thing.

After all, nobody had helped Bridie and her mother when *they* were on the way to the poorhouse. Certainly Mrs. Kigley and Lavinia wouldn't have helped. . . .

Bridie brought herself up short. It didn't matter what Mrs. Kigley and Lavinia would have done. What mattered was what Bridie would have done. Surely she could be kinder than a Kigley.

Maybe the Kigleys could get jobs. It ought to be possible for a woman and girl, together, to work hard enough to stay out of the poorhouse.

Of course, if Mrs. Kigley got a job, her husband would go and collect her wages. He would collect Lavinia's, too. That was how Bridie and her mother had ended up in the poorhouse.

If only Bridie's mother hadn't remarried, she and Bridie could have made it.

When Bridie got to the Wesleyan Chapel, it was even more crowded than the day before. Fans fluttered. The Declaration of Sentiments was being read and discussed, item by item.

Bridie carried the basket of sandwiches and cakes up and set them behind the chairs near the podium. Mrs. Stanton was at the podium.

"Next item," Mrs. Stanton announced. She looked down at the Declaration of Sentiments, and then up at the audience. " 'He has taken from her all right in property, even to the wages she earns.' "

Bridie froze, just like she had last night at dinner. Only this time it was her mother that she saw: Bridie and her mother headed to the poorhouse, walking a line of light in a dark, uncaring world.

A man in the audience stood up. "Well, actually—"

Mr. Mott stepped up beside Mrs. Stanton. "The chair recognizes Mr. Ansel Bascom."

Mr. Bascom was a frightfully important man, a politician, and the owner of the apple orchard where the Fourth of July picnic was held—the orchard that the Cayugas had planted.

"Actually," said Mr. Bascom, "thanks to the Married Women's Property Act, which I worked hard to pass in Albany this year, women in New York State do now have the right to control their own property if they inherit it or if it is given to them."

Mr. Bascom went on talking for quite a while. Bridie looked around her at the people in the hall. There were men and women, all of them people who didn't have to go to work today, a Thursday. Probably a lot of them didn't have to work *any* day. There were boys and girls. There was Mr. Bascom's daughter, sitting in the pew beside where he stood. She had white ruffles on her pantalets. There were no other girls with just stockings in the church. Bridie was the only one. As far as girls were concerned, it was strictly a white-pantalets meeting.

"I beg your pardon," said Mrs. Stanton when Mr. Bascom paused for breath, "but the new law does not include a married woman's wages. Those still belong to her husband."

"Granted," said Mr. Bascom. "But since a woman, having chosen her husband, can surely trust him to expend those wages—"

"BALDERDASH!" yelled Bridie.

There were gasps amid a stunned silence. Every eye in the chapel was turned on Bridie. Even Mr. Bascom halted in mid-flow.

Bridie wished, oh how she wished, that her Bump of Cautiousness wasn't merely a hollow. She knew she was in disgrace. She was about to get thrown out of the chapel. Quite possibly she was about to lose her job.

And she might get arrested for swearing, too. A girl could say *fiddlesticks*, but *balderdash?*

She took a step toward the door, ready to flee, when the chairman's voice rang into the silence.

"The chair recognizes Miss Phoebe"—he turned to Mrs. Stanton, who murmured Bridie's last name to him—"Gallagher."

All eyes turned to Bridie again, but this time they looked interested.

"Well, um." Bridie had to think of something to say, and fast. "Sometimes a woman's husband maybe isn't all he could be, and—"

"Louder," said several people, and "Can't hear you!"

Bridie stepped in front of the pulpit, where they could all see her, the only girl there that wasn't wearing white pantalets.

She remembered what boys had been taught about public speaking, in the schools she'd attended. She'd overheard the teacher telling the boys to talk to the back of the room. Bridie put her head back and looked at the people ranged around the gallery on three sides of the room. She tried to make her voice go up to the gallery.

"If a woman is working," she said, "then she's making, um, money that's hers. *She's* the one that worked for it. And it could be that she wants to share it with her husband, but it could also be that he's . . . um, that things aren't going well, and that she needs to support herself and her children."

She looked around. Everyone in the whole vast crowd was listening to her. She clutched the pebble in her pocket and took a deep breath. "But even if her husband is drunk, or beats her, or is never there at all, he can still come around to the factory—or wherever she works, I mean—on payday, and the boss gives her pay envelope to him."

Still listening.

"Then the husband goes off again, and maybe he gets drunk or something with the money, without giving his wife or his children anything."

She turned and looked directly at Mr. Bascom. "Maybe that's not the way it's supposed to be, but sometimes it's the way it is, and the law shouldn't allow it. But it does."

She looked back at Mr. Mott, the chairman. "I think I'm done."

Mr. Mott nodded at her.

Mr. Bascom made a slight bow in her direction. "I concede the point."

And that was it! The sky didn't fall. The earth didn't swallow Bridie up. The conversation simply went on. Mr. Douglass stood up and said, "I should like to observe that had women the right to vote, such questions as diverting their wages to an errant husband would not even arise."

Mrs. Mott stood up and said, "Fre— Mr. Douglass, I hardly feel that Woman need enter into the political fray to secure her religious, civil, and social rights."

"Pray, how else is she to do it? In this denial of the right to participate in government," said Mr. Douglass, "not merely the degradation of woman and the perpetuation of a great injustice happens, but the maiming and repudiation of one-half of the moral and intellectual power of the government of the world."

Highfalutin talk. Bridie couldn't keep up with it. Many other people rose at the same time and started to talk, and Mr. Mott banged his gavel and called for order as Bridie hurried out of the church.

She had almost made it to the door when a woman she didn't know grabbed her by the arm.

"Thee spoke well," said the stranger. "I think

thee has carried the point, and that there will be no more argument against that particular item."

"Thank you," said Bridie, curtsying, and fled.

⚜

The convention ended that evening. The next morning, all of Mrs. Stanton's guests left. As everyone was packing up, Bridie heard about what had happened. All the items in the Declaration of Sentiments had been approved, including the one Bridie had spoken for.

The one that had given the most trouble was the resolution that women should have the right to vote. "Frederick turned the tide there," said Mrs. Post. "After he spoke, the measure passed."

"Barely," said Mr. Douglass, hoarsely. "And too soon after my tonsil surgery." He touched his throat.

And then the convention had voted to approve the Declaration of Sentiments. After that, one hundred people had signed it. Sixty-eight women had signed, and then thirty-two men.

And what did that mean?

Nothing, as far as Bridie could tell. It was just a convention in a little mill town in York State. It didn't *change* anything.

It didn't mean that Rose could be a scientist, or

that Bridie could be a printer. It didn't stop a man from collecting his wife's wages, and it didn't mean Mrs. Stanton could jump in a coach decorated with pine boughs and ride down to the polls to vote.

"But it means they know what they're fighting for," said Rose. "They've spelled it all out in black-and-white."

"So what happens next?"

Rose admitted she didn't know.

16

A MOST UNWELCOME VISITOR

Rose had been hired again, to help clean up after all the guests left. The girls were upstairs dragging sheets off the beds. Bridie looked out the window and saw Mr. Kigley coming up Bayard Street in his wagon.

Bridie stood at the window, sheets in hand. Surely he was headed for the free bridge and home.

The wagon turned onto Washington Street, coming right toward the house.

"That's him," said Bridie to Rose, who had joined her at the window.

"Maybe he's going to the flour mill," said Rose, sounding like she didn't think he was.

"He doesn't have any grain sacks with him."

And indeed he stopped before the house, hitched Dobbin to a hitching post, and started climbing the steps.

Bridie and Rose crept down the stairs as quietly as they could. They stopped at the landing where the stair turned. From there they could see the front door. Mrs. Stanton was at her writing desk.

There was a loud, demanding knock on the door.

Mrs. Stanton got up and went to open it. Bridie could only see her whalebone-stiffened back, but it was clear from the way she said "Yes?" that she was not happy to see anyone of Mr. Kigley's description on her doorstep.

"You Mrs. Shtanton? Lemme talk to your huzhband."

"You, sir, are the worse for drink." Mrs. Stanton started to close the door.

Mr. Kigley put his foot in it. "Where'sh your huzhband, woman! Want to talk to him."

"And yet I am certain he does not want to talk to you. Be off!"

Rose and Bridie exchanged a glance. Mr. Stanton wasn't home. He was probably on a train somewhere. Bridie had only ever seen him once, as he passed through on his way from one speaking engagement to another.

Mr. Kigley suddenly pushed at the door, and Mrs. Stanton pushed back. Her feet started to slide slowly across the bare wooden floor as the door inched inward. Bridie and Rose rushed down the stairs and threw their weight at the door, trying to stop its inexorable opening. Six-year-old Neil came running in from the parlor and pushed with them.

Bridie felt the door vibrate as Mr. Kigley kicked and pounded on it.

They kept pushing, struggling against the shaking door.

Finally it snicked shut, and Mrs. Stanton threw the latch.

"I had word you're conshealing my wife and child on these premishes!" Mr. Kigley yelled through the door. "They're mine and I mean to have 'em back!"

"Back door," Rose murmured, and darted off to latch it.

"I am sending word to the constable right now," Mrs. Stanton said to Mr. Kigley through the door. Her tone was steely and firm. "And if you are anywhere on my property when he arrives, then I will have you arrested for trespassing."

Mr. Kigley delivered himself of some opinions about the constable.

"*And* for swearing," said Mrs. Stanton. "Be off!"

There was silence from the other side of the door.

Bridie went to the window and looked out. Mr. Kigley was unhitching Dobbin. He climbed onto the wagon seat, shook the reins, and drove away.

"He's gone," she told the others.

Rose looked as shaken as Bridie felt. Mrs. Stanton didn't look shaken. She looked ready to ride into battle.

"Do you want me to go for the constable, Ma?" said Neil.

"Not yet," said Mrs. Stanton. "Not until I understand what is going on in my own house. *Am* I concealing his wife and child on my premises?"

She looked at Bridie and Rose, but it was Neil who answered. "They're in the washhouse, Ma."

Bridie looked at him in surprise. She was impressed that he'd found them and known not to tell anyone.

"They're mean," he added. "I don't like them."

"They thought Mr. Kigley was going to kill them," said Bridie.

"I'm not at all surprised," said Mrs. Stanton. "But, Phoebe, aren't these the people you ran away from? How did they force you to take them in?"

"They didn't," said Bridie.

"Then why—"

"You have to help people that need help," said Rose.

Bridie nodded agreement.

"I suppose." Mrs. Stanton sighed.

"Now shall I go for the constable?" said Neil.

"No," said Mrs. Stanton. "Because the constable is quite likely to side with Mr. Kigley."

"But—" said Bridie.

"Not so much on the matter of the wife," said Mrs. Stanton. "While the law doesn't exactly *allow* a wife to flee, it no longer returns her to her husband when she does. The child is another matter. He has the right to her labor until she turns eighteen or marries."

"Or he kills her," said Bridie.

"I had better go and talk to this woman myself," said Mrs. Stanton. "And then I shall have to think."

"Am I out of a job?" said Bridie.

"What? No. No, of course not." Mrs. Stanton gave her a hard look. "You did the right thing, Phoebe. I want you to remember that. Because it's likely that certain people are going to tell you that you did the wrong thing."

※

Rose stood beside Mr. Davis's desk and opened her arithmetic book. "I started the addition of vulgar fractions, teacher."

Mr. Davis took the book from her and peered at it. "Very well. What's one-fourth plus two-thirds, Rose?"

"Eleven-twelfths," said Rose. "But I don't understand why. . . ."

"Well, because that's the answer, Rose," said Mr. Davis.

And Rose had the feeling, as she did more and more often, that Mr. Davis was in over his aching head.

"I think you've learned enough to go on by yourself from here," said Mr. Davis.

"But—"

"There are only two weeks left in the summer term, and I shall be seeking employment elsewhere."

Rose felt her stomach drop. It was what she'd been dreading. "But you'll be back for winter term?"

She tried not to sound like she was pleading.

"No, they . . ." Mr. Davis seemed to change his mind about what he'd been going to say. "I have decided not to teach in the winter."

"Because of the big boys?" Rose knew she

shouldn't talk about this. "Mr. Davis, they don't come every winter! And you could move to a school closer to the center of town, they're not as bad there. . . ."

She trailed off. She knew she was not making things better.

"I wish to return to my native Boston," said Mr. Davis coldly. "But there will be another teacher coming."

Yes; the school board would find a teacher who could fight the big boys, Rose thought. Schoolteachers who taught in the winter had to be men, and iron-fisted men at that.

It wasn't *fair*!

So much wasn't fair.

"Carry on studying your arithmetic, Rose, and perhaps the next teacher will be able to help you further with it."

"If he even lets me come to school," Rose couldn't help saying, bitterly.

"If he does not, you must seek farther afield," said Mr. Davis. "I have no doubt you can do it. You are clever and determined, a credit to your race."

And with that he stood up to go, and Rose had to go too. A credit to her race. That was not what she wanted to be. She wanted to be a scientist. That was for the future. For now, what she wanted was a teacher who knew mathematics and who couldn't be taken away from her by complaining parents and big boys.

17

MR. STANTON DOES NOT APPROVE.

Bridie took bowls of hasty pudding and some wrinkled, last-year's apples out to the washhouse.

"We have to actually do wash tomorrow," she told Mrs. Kigley.

"Speak when spoken to," said Mrs. Kigley, taking her bowl of pudding and turning up her nose at the apples. "Where do you expect us to hide while you do the wash?"

"Maybe you could help," said Bridie.

"And be *seen?*"

"He already knows you're here," Bridie reminded her.

Mrs. Kigley sniffed. "Mrs. Stanton said he was not to be admitted onto the property."

It had been several days since the scene with Mr. Kigley. Mrs. Stanton had returned from her interview with Mrs. Kigley and Lavinia that day looking grim and had said that she certainly wouldn't want that woman in her *house*.

"If I had the money," said Mrs. Kigley, "I'd go to my sister's in Rochester."

"I thought you didn't have anywhere to go."

"Well, I have my sister in Rochester," said Mrs. Kigley, in tones that suggested that any idiot would have known this.

A ticket to Rochester cost more than Bridie made in a week. Even if she'd had the money, she wouldn't give it to the Kigleys.

She would dearly love to be rid of them, though.

※

"Well, here's a fine thing!" said Mrs. Stanton. "There's going to be another convention, in Rochester!"

She was at her desk, opening her mail. Bridie was sitting on the floor, reading the younger boys a book Mr. Douglass had brought them from Rochester: *The Anti-Slavery Alphabet.*

" 'P is the Parent, sorrowing / And weeping all alone,' " Bridie read. " 'The child he loved to lean upon—' "

"Just think, another convention, two weeks after the first! Perhaps the nation really is ready for our message," said Mrs. Stanton.

Bridie waited to see if this was going to require some response.

Gat pushed the book at her. "More!"

" '. . . His only son is gone.' " Bridie stopped to let the boys trace the big Q and R with their fingers. Then she went on reading.

Meanwhile, Mrs. Stanton was opening more letters. Newspaper clippings fell out. She spread them on her desk and scrutinized each in turn.

" 'S is for Sugar that the slave / Is toiling hard to make / To put into your pie and tea / Your coffee and your cake.' "

"*We* only have anti-slavery sugar," said Kit.

"Yes, I know, but the book is telling people who don't know about anti-slavery sugar," Bridie explained.

"Oh dear," said Mrs. Stanton.

Bridie looked up. Mrs. Stanton seemed suddenly discouraged. One of the boys shoved the book at Bridie again, but she got up and went over to see what was bothering her.

Mrs. Stanton was staring at the papers in front of her.

One was a letter. In all capital letters it said: WHY DO YOU HATE MEN YOU WULD DIE IF IT WERNT FOR MEN YOUR A MAN-HATER. There was no signature.

But Mrs. Stanton didn't seem particularly upset about that one.

She pointed at a clipping. "This one's from one of the Rochester papers. They call my ideas 'impractical, absurd, and ridiculous.'"

"They're not!" said Bridie.

"They say we 'seemed to be really in earnest'! Goodness, I wonder what gave them that idea," said Mrs. Stanton bitterly.

Bridie didn't know what to say. Mrs. Stanton looked dejected.

"Listen to this one: 'A woman is nobody. A wife is everything. A pretty girl is equal to ten thousand men. . . .' Don't they understand that that's the problem?"

"But, Mrs. Stanton—"

"And this one—'The most shocking and unnatural event ever recorded in the history of womanity!' Womanity, Phoebe!"

"But there's the convention in Rochester coming up," said Bridie.

"I don't know if I should even go. It's expensive, and I'd have to leave the boys with my sister, and . . ." She trailed off.

"But you could take the Kigleys to Rochester and get rid of them," said Bridie encouragingly.

"I've been trying to raise the money for that," said Mrs. Stanton. "It's a cause no one is interested in."

"Oh." Bridie hadn't known that. "Because they don't like the Kigleys?"

"Because they think I have no business interfering between man and wife," said Mrs. Stanton. "Well, never mind. I suppose I won't go. Go back to what you were doing, Phoebe."

"Mrs. Stanton, you know that one thing in your Declaration about how a husband shouldn't have the right to collect his wife's wages?" said Bridie.

"Oh yes, there's a newspaper clipping mocking that here somewhere."

"When we first came here from Ireland," said Bridie, "it was just my mother and me, because my father and brothers had died in the Hunger. My mother married an Erie Canal boatman, because she figured as how it would be easier in a new country if she had a husband and all."

Mrs. Stanton looked slightly less despondent; she sensed a fight in the air.

"Then he brought us to Seneca Falls and got us work in the woolen mill—"

"A fine anti-slavery manufactory," said Mrs. Stanton. "They use no cotton."

"Maybe so, but John Gerry—that's my mother's husband—told the foreman to hold our pay envelopes until he was in town. He'd only show up every few weeks, and then he'd collect them and go on a spree."

Now Mrs. Stanton definitely sensed battle. "What! And he gave you nothing?"

"He gave us a little bit, but we had to beg him for it, and it was never enough to live on. And then Mother got sick and she said as how she wasn't going to work sick just so he could go on a spree, and I couldn't make enough for us to get on with even if I would have been allowed to keep it—"

"Which you should have been," said Mrs. Stanton. "The law does exempt your pay from his clutches, as you are not his born child. I shall go down and talk to the foreman about that!"

The fight was definitely back in Mrs. Stanton now.

"So we ended up in the poorhouse," Bridie said. "And then she died."

Mrs. Stanton looked incensed.

"And I don't want that to ever happen to anybody again," said Bridie. "People ought to have the right to their own pay envelope no matter who they are."

"They certainly should!"

"And think of Rose, she wants to be a scientist, but the schools—"

Just then there came a knock at the door.

Bridie went and opened it. It was a woman who had been at the convention; Bridie didn't know her name.

The woman and Mrs. Stanton went into the next room and sat on the sofa.

"Elizabeth, you've got to take my name off that Declaration of yours!" said the woman.

"But you signed—"

"I made a mistake. People are laughing at us!"

And Mrs. Stanton, with the fight newly awakened in her, proceeded to talk the woman out of taking her name off the Declaration.

Bridie went back to reading to the boys. "'U is for Upper Canada / Where the poor slave has found / Rest after all his wanderings / For it is British ground!'"

Mr. Stanton came home. Bridie was in the kitchen when he arrived. Nancy, the cook, had gone home to the Flats and Bridie was up to her elbows in dish suds.

"Here we are, Lizzie, my love!" she heard him say, out in the parlor. "And how are you and the kiddies?"

The boys came pouring down the stairs. "Papa!"

Bridie felt a pang. The things she kept locked away inside her head crept out just for a minute, and she thought of her brothers as Mr. Stanton gave the boys a new ball he'd brought for them. She thought of her parents as he kissed Mrs. Stanton.

She was alone in the world, and a long way from Ireland.

"I've brought the most interesting newspaper from California—here, my love, I think you'll find it amusing. These crazy rumors about gold . . ."

Then he looked up and saw Bridie watching from the kitchen door. "And here's something for you, Phoebe."

Bridie dried her hands on her apron and took the hair ribbon he handed her. Green, the color of Ireland. Bridie hadn't expected to be remembered. She suddenly felt tearful.

"And what have you been up to while I've been gone, my dear?" he asked Mrs. Stanton.

"Oh, women's rights," said Mrs. Stanton.

"And very sensible too," said Mr. Stanton. "As long as you stay away from that nonsense of women voting. No one will listen to you if you keep harping on that; it makes the whole thing ridiculous."

Bridie went back to the dishes. She shaved some more soap into the water with a knife, then used a straw whisk to stir up more suds. Through the doorway she heard Mr. Stanton telling them about his journey, all the speeches he'd made for the Free Soil Party, how he'd be leaving again tomorrow to make more speeches and then head on to the party convention in Buffalo, where it was expected that they would nominate Martin Van Buren for president.

"Not a choice I approve of," Mr. Stanton said. "Van Buren has already been president, and one cannot forget that he wanted to hand the *Amistad* captives over to slave traders. But he is against slavery spreading to the new territories we've acquired from Mexico, so he's the man we need right now, I suppose."

Bridie scraped at a bit of egg stuck to a plate. She heard no further mention of the women's rights convention.

"It stands to reason, though," Mr. Stanton went on. "The country is divided over slavery, and getting more so every day. If we were ever to elect a real abolitionist president, it would end in civil war."

"Oh, surely not," said Mrs. Stanton.

"Papa, there are ladies in the washhouse," said four-year-old Kit suddenly.

"Doing the wash in the middle of the night, are they?" said Mr. Stanton, sounding amused.

"They're *hiding*," said Kit.

Bridie came to the kitchen door again to watch.

Mr. Stanton turned to Mrs. Stanton. "Passengers? The washhouse is too visible. Why don't you have them down in the cellar?"

Bridie watched Mrs. Stanton take a deep breath. "They're not passengers. It's a woman and her child."

"But not Underground Railroad passengers?" Mr. Stanton looked perplexed, but still amused. "Tell me this riddle."

Mrs. Stanton explained. As she did, Mr. Stanton looked less and less amused.

"You have gone too far, Lizzie," he said, when she finished.

"They feared for their lives," said Mrs. Stanton, surprisingly mildly. "A woman and a child have a right not to be beaten."

"Nobody has the right to interfere between man and wife, Lizzie."

"If they were slaves running from a cruel master who had beaten them, you wouldn't say I didn't have the right to interfere," said Mrs. Stanton.

"It would be entirely a different matter. This woman chose her husband, freely, of her own will. Let no man put them asunder!"

"Lavinia didn't choose him," Bridie heard herself say.

Mr. Stanton looked at her. "I see the whole household is united on the matter. I'll go and see the husband in the morning and—"

"Henry, you cannot," said Mrs. Stanton. "He's a drunkard and a thoroughly unreasonable man."

"We should at least hear his side of it."

"Don't you even want to hear their side of it first?" said Bridie. She knew she should be seen and not heard, but her bump of cautiousness hadn't gotten any bigger.

"They're mean," said six-year-old Neil. "But he's mean too. I think he might be meaner."

Mr. Stanton sighed. "Well, do they at least have plans to move on? We can't keep them here, not in defiance of the husband's wishes."

"Mrs. Kigley has a sister in Rochester," said Bridie.

Mrs. Stanton shot Bridie a look, and Mr. Stanton

did not look pleased. A sister in Rochester was still coming between man and wife.

"I haven't the strength to argue; I've been arguing for the last three weeks," he said. "And I'll get on a train and go off to argue some more tomorrow. We'll talk about it in the morning."

He started up the stairs, with the little boys following him. Mrs. Stanton looked after him, then said under her breath, "It's my house, after all."

By the time Mr. Stanton left for the station the next day, the decision had apparently been made that the Kigleys were to be taken to Rochester, and Mrs. Stanton would pay for their tickets herself.

18

MRS. KIGLEY'S ESCAPE

The boys had been sent to stay with their aunt. Mrs. Stanton was to take the train to Rochester with Lavinia and Mrs. Kigley. Mrs. Stanton had hired Solomon Butler, the teamster, to take them to the station in his wagon.

Mr. Butler also worked with the Underground Railroad. Bridie had the impression that most of the people of color in Seneca Falls did.

Now the trick was to get to the train station without Mr. Kigley finding out.

Rose and Bridie were to act as scouts for the mission. They would walk some way ahead and behind, looking around for any sign of Mr. Kigley.

175

Rose went in front. She hurried along Bayard Street fifty yards ahead of the wagon, keeping an eye out in all directions.

Bridie ran just as far behind, turning every few seconds to see if Mr. Kigley was coming up the road from the lake.

Rose reached the bridge and signaled that it was clear. Bridie signaled back that no one was following.

They crossed the bridge, first Rose, then the wagon, then Bridie.

From the bridge she could see up and down the river and the canal—no trace of Mr. Kigley. Just boats and barges and factories.

Rose was up on Fall Street now, signaling down that all was still clear. Bridie signaled back—all clear here, too.

Mr. Butler's horses pulled the wagon up onto Fall Street. Rose had run ahead to scout out State Street. Bridie looked back the way they'd come—uh-oh.

Was that Mr. Kigley on the bridge?

Bridie froze, her heart thumping. She shaded her eyes against the sun and looked again. No, it was just someone who looked like him. Whew.

By the time she started up State Street, past the

house where Rose boarded, Rose was already signaling from the train station that it was safe.

The wagon arrived at the station and everyone tumbled out. The metal-capped wooden rails were already singing with the vibrations of the approaching train.

"It's an express," Mrs. Stanton was saying when Bridie arrived. "There are no more station stops before Rochester, and it goes nearly fifteen miles an hour! We'll—"

The rest of what she said Bridie couldn't hear, as the train thundered into the station, smoke and sparks pouring from its smokestack. It gasped to a stop.

The door of a passenger car swung open. "All aboard for Rochester!"

Then several things happened very quickly.

Mrs. Stanton picked up her valise, gathered her skirts, mounted the steps, and squeezed her impractical clothes through the door of the train car.

Suddenly Mr. Kigley jumped out from behind a stack of barrels and made a grab at Mrs. Kigley, who leapt and scrambled into the train car.

Lavinia ran the opposite way from her mother, fleeing toward State Street as the train started with a lurch.

Mr. Kigley ran after Lavinia. Rose stuck a foot out and tripped him.

Mr. Kigley hit the stone railroad platform with a sickening smack. Bridie heard this behind her, because she and Rose were already running too.

Bridie and Rose caught up with Lavinia. They couldn't hear any feet pursuing behind them yet.

Rose grabbed Lavinia. "In here, quick!"

She led both of them into Mr. Moody's boarding house. She locked the door behind them. All three girls sat down on a bench and leaned back against the long dining table, out of breath.

"They've gone to Rochester without me," said Lavinia. "And he's going to kill me."

Bridie didn't want to sympathize, but it was hard not to. Lavinia looked really scared.

"I bet he saw me come in here," said Lavinia. "He has to have seen me come in here; it's right down the street. . . . Whose house is this anyway? Isn't this where all those colored people live?"

"Shut up," Bridie suggested.

"What am I going to *do!*"

Rose and Bridie exchanged a glance. Neither of them liked Lavinia even a little bit. On the other hand, they could hardly let Mr. Kigley catch her. It was possible he really would kill her.

"Maybe her mother will come back for her," said Rose without much hope.

"The train doesn't stop before Rochester," said Bridie. "And coming back would cost money she doesn't have."

They sat and thought in silence while Lavinia wrung her hands.

"Mr. Douglass did say I could come and stay with them in Rochester," said Rose thoughtfully. "And go to school."

"*We* don't have money to get to Rochester!" said Bridie.

"There's more than one way to get to Rochester," said Rose.

19

ANOTHER WAY TO ROCHESTER

The three girls ran along the towpath of the Cayuga & Seneca Canal. Rose and Bridie had had to argue with Lavinia to get her to see sense: it was no good waiting around the train station now that her father knew she was there. They'd slipped out the back door of the boarding house, hurried through backyards and alleys to the Flats, and crossed the catwalk over the factories to get to the towpath of the Cayuga & Seneca Canal.

Mr. Moody, Rose's landlord, was a boatman, and he had just left on a voyage that morning, bound for the Erie Canal and Buffalo. The boat would pass right through Rochester.

Rose thought they might be able to catch up with him, if they hurried. The boats only moved as fast as the mules pulling them could walk, and they had to stop to go through locks—and at one point for the mules to cross the canal on a towpath bridge.

The girls dodged past slow-moving mule teams and their drivers, being careful not to get too close behind a mule so that they wouldn't get kicked. Lavinia skidded in a mule plop and fell, sprawling. Rose and Bridie dragged her to her feet, and they ran on, past barges and boats and canoes.

When they finally caught up with Mr. Moody's barge, it had just entered a lock. The lockkeeper and his wife were using the long lever beams to shut the doors of the lock behind the barge. The barge's towrope had been unhitched and the mule driver—called a hoggee, Bridie remembered—was leading the mules along to the other side of the lock to wait.

"Mr. Moody!" Rose called.

Mr. Moody stood on the bow of the boat. He waved to Rose as if she was just saying good morning.

Rose waved both arms. "Mr. Moody, let us on, please!"

He didn't seem to understand. Probably he couldn't hear them over the sound of the water rushing out as the lockkeepers slowly opened the gate ahead of them, lowering the water level in the lock.

Bridie looked back frantically to see if Mr. Kigley was chasing them. But she couldn't see past the mule teams coming along the path.

Bridie and Rose seized the rope by which the barge was tied up, and tried to pull it toward them.

Finally Mr. Moody seemed to get the point. He grabbed a plank, swung it across the gap between the boat and the lock wall, and held it while Rose hurried across.

Bridie saw Rose urgently explaining something to him.

"Go across," Bridie told Lavinia.

"I might fall in!"

"I might push you in," said Bridie, thoroughly fed up with the girl and her whining.

Giving her a poisonous look, Lavinia got onto the plank and inched her way carefully across. Bridie followed, and then she dragged the plank back onto the boat—Rose and Mr. Moody were too busy arguing to help, and Lavinia was being Lavinia.

The canal boat was seventy feet long, with an enclosed cabin stretching most of its length, so that the freight wouldn't get wet. There was a deck at each end.

"What good is this?" said Lavinia. "We're stuck here now. This boat isn't going anywhere."

"We have to wait till the water in the lock is down to the level of the next section of the canal," said Bridie, trying to be patient. "That's how canals work. You go through locks, so that it's flat the whole way."

The water level had already dropped a few feet as the water rushed out of the gate ahead of them.

"All the way to Rochester?" Mr. Moody was saying.

"She has an aunt there," said Rose.

"And who's paying for this?" But Bridie could see from Mr. Moody's expression that he had already given in. "You'd better get inside," he said to Lavinia.

Lavinia seemed about to complain, then Mr. Moody held open the door to the cabin and gave Lavinia a look, and she went.

The stone walls of the lock rose higher and higher on both sides as the water level went down. The smell of muddy water and algae rose. Now the barge was so far down in the lock that Bridie had to tilt her head back to see the top of the wall. . . . There, she could see a man's boots, far above her.

She looked up farther. The boots contained Mr.

Kigley, who was standing on the edge of the lock, looking down at her.

As she stared in dismay, he turned and walked away.

The water stopped rushing through the gate. The gate was fully open. The canal barges drifted forward to where the mules waited . . . and Mr. Kigley waited, too.

Bridie exchanged a horrified glance with Rose.

Meanwhile, the adults were talking. There were several other boatmen in the crew, as well as the cook, Mrs. Moggy. They were all in a huddle with Ferris Moody, discussing the situation.

"We might as well change mule teams here and deal with him right now."

"But this team's only been on for a couple hours."

"Close enough."

The boatmen went to the stern of the boat. Bridie and Rose clambered up onto the cabin roof and ran along it to the rear deck, where the spare mules were kept in a stable. From there they watched as the men dragged out a wide, mule-strong gangplank. It looked much sturdier than the narrow board the girls had crossed.

Bridie looked at Rose. Were the boatmen going to let Mr. Kigley onto the boat?

"I *told* them . . . ," Rose murmured.

But had they listened? Bridie remembered how Mrs. Stanton's husband had sided with Mr. Kigley—or almost sided with him. Would the boatmen feel the same way?

The girls watched and waited, nervous.

Mr. Kigley eyed the gangplank, and the men on the boat eyed him. They did not lay the gangplank down.

"That's my daughter you got there. Bring her back, you kidnappers!" said Mr. Kigley.

Lavinia was still hiding in the cabin.

Mr. Moody looked up at the cabin roof. "Is either of you girls his daughter?"

Rose and Bridie shook their heads emphatically.

The second mule team—most canal boats had two—was being led out of the stable by the second hoggee.

"*That* one's mine too," said Mr. Kigley, pointing at Bridie.

"No, I'm not," said Bridie, trying to keep her voice calm. She was both terrified and furious. "I was at your house and I left. It was my right to leave. You've got nothing to do with me."

"We're going to put the gangplank across," one of the boatmen called to the hoggee onshore.

The hoggee onshore, standing beside his mules, nodded. He pursed his lips and waited just a second, as though thinking things through. Then he turned around and punched Mr. Kigley in the nose.

Mr. Kigley tried to hit the hoggee, but the man ducked and kicked his feet out from under him. Mr. Kigley scrambled up again.

While the two men were fighting, the hoggee on the boat brought the fresh team clop-clopping across the gangplank, onto shore. He calmly unhitched the old team, hitched up the fresh team, and led the old team back to the barge.

The second mule in the old team did not want to come aboard. It stopped with its front hooves down in the boat, its hind hooves up on the gangplank, and its rear end sticking up in the air.

The hoggee coaxed. He urged. The men on the boat grabbed the mule's bridle and pulled. The hoggee threatened and cursed. The mule stayed where she was.

Then Mr. Kigley broke free of the hoggee he was fighting. He charged across the gangplank, coming toward the mule from behind.

Everyone watching knew this was a very, very bad idea. Rose winced. Bridie covered her eyes.

There was a muffled *THUNK* as the mule let fly

with one hoof, kicking Mr. Kigley in the midriff and sending him flying through the air to land in a heap on the bank.

"Is he dead?" Bridie asked.

"No, he's moving," said Rose.

Bridie uncovered her eyes. The mule was calmly walking into her stall, the gangplank was up, and the barge was moving on.

20

THE ERIE CANAL

The barge glided on, at a slow-plodding mule's pace, north through the Montezuma Marsh to the great Erie Canal, where they turned west toward Rochester and Buffalo.

The girls kept an anxious watch for Mr. Kigley, in case he reappeared. Lavinia eventually emerged from the cabin. This was not an improvement, but Rose and Bridie resolved to enjoy the trip anyway. They sat up on top of the cabin and peeled vegetables for the cook. After they'd done that, they got out and walked for a while along the towpath, and petted the mules, Mephistopheles and Sally.

The placid green water lay still, except for the occasional wakes of the slow-moving barges and packet boats. The canal was wide enough for passing, but there was only one towpath. So whenever two mule teams met, one was unhitched and stood aside for the other to pass.

Everyone sat on the roof to eat the Irish stew Mrs. Moggy had prepared. Everything tasted better when you ate it outdoors, Bridie thought, but the stew would've tasted good anywhere. It was nothing like anything she'd ever had in Ireland.

"What is this stuff?" said Lavinia, poking at the stew in her bowl and wrinkling her nose.

"This is delicious," said Bridie loudly.

"Low bridge!" called out Mr. Moody, and everyone set their bowls down and scrambled off the roof.

When the bridge was past, they were relieved to see their bowls were still there. Sometimes low bridges were very, very low.

After dinner, Rose managed to get Lavinia to help wash the dishes.

Night fell, and the girls borrowed hay from the mules and made a place to sleep on deck. Bridie looked up at the stars and waited for Lavinia to stop grumbling.

Another barge drifted past, and someone on it was plucking on a banjo. The boatmen on their barge picked up the song:

We were forty miles from Albany, forget I never
shall
What a terrible storm we had one night on the
E-ri-e Canal.
Well the Erie was a-rising, and the rum was
getting low
And I scarcely think we'll get a drink till we
get to Buffalo.

Erie Canal barges traveled day and night to make the long journey across the state in just nine days. Mr. Moody was working this trip all the way west to Buffalo, then back east again and down the Cayuga & Seneca Canal to Seneca Falls. He told the girls they would probably reach Rochester early in the morning of the day after tomorrow.

A few times in the night the girls were awakened by the rush of water filling a lock. Now that they were westward bound, the locks lifted the boat higher for each new section of canal. Bridie fell back asleep to the sound of the mules clopping across the gangplank.

The next day dawned, with birdsong and a faint, drizzling rain. Farms and villages slid past. Bridie and Rose stood on the bow of the barge to yell "Low bridge!" whenever one came into sight, and once "Really low bridge!" when they thought the roof of the cabin might scrape . . . and it did.

Rose pored over a copy of that same newspaper Mr. Stanton had brought home, the one from California. One of the boatmen had lent it to her.

"It looks like it's really true about the gold," she told Bridie. "They've found gold in California at a place called the American River."

Lavinia grabbed the paper away from Rose and read, while Rose looked offended and Lavinia didn't notice.

"It's a load of hogwash, if you ask me," said Lavinia.

"Which no one did," Bridie pointed out. She grabbed the paper from Lavinia and started to read.

"Supposing they did find gold in California, why would they tell everybody back east about it?" said Lavinia.

"The paper's for Californians," said Rose.

"It says it's a special edition for back east," said Bridie.

"They're up to something, those Californians," said Lavinia.

Bridie handed the paper back to Rose. She didn't know what she thought. Those rumors about gold in California had been going around for months. Bridie hadn't paid much attention. California was a long way away.

But they had printing presses out there, too, it seemed. And so the story about gold had traveled through time and space to York State, riding on a piece of paper. That was what print could do.

Bridie wondered who had set the type.

"I think it's true about the gold," said Rose. "Why would everyone be talking about it if it wasn't? Besides, it's all here in this paper."

"How far away is California?" Bridie was still a bit uncertain of American geography.

"About three thousand miles," said Rose.

"That's as far as Ireland!" said Bridie.

"And harder to get to," said Rose. "Because you have to go across land, with oxen and stuff, and people get dysentery and cholera, and this one wagon train a couple years ago got stuck in the snow and they all *ate* each other."

"It doesn't seem worthwhile," said Bridie.

"There are mountains in California, and big grizzly bears. And monstrous huge trees, like nowhere else in the world, and earthquakes."

That did sound rather appealing.

Lavinia sneered and took herself off to the other end of the boat.

"What's going to happen when we get to Rochester?" said Bridie.

"We'll go to Mr. Douglass's newspaper," said Rose. "He'll know where to find Mrs. Stanton and she'll know where to find Lavinia's mother."

"And then . . ." Bridie trailed off. She knew Rose wanted to continue her schooling.

"He did say I could stay with them," said Rose.

"Do the Douglasses have a really big house?"

"Normal sized I think."

Bridie touched the pebble in her pocket. She was still a long way from Ireland, but she no longer felt so alone. She had Rose for a friend. If Rose moved to Rochester, Bridie would be alone again.

You couldn't really count Mrs. Stanton. She was kind. All the Stantons were, even the tiny ones. But Bridie was just a servant in their house, and they had had a lot of servants.

Bridie wanted what was best for Rose, of course.

You had to want that, didn't you, for your friends? Bridie wasn't sure where her bump of friendship was, but she could feel it telling her that.

Well, they could stay friends, anyway, even if they were going to be a long way apart—couldn't they?

"If you keep going on the Erie Canal to the end, then you can get on a ship and go across the Great Lakes to Chicago and even further," said Rose.

"What's Chicago?" said Bridie.

"The fastest-growing city in the world. It was hardly even there when we were born." Rose looked down at the passing water. "And there are even more places further west. I'd like to go someday."

It was really true, Bridie thought. Starting from Seneca Falls, you could go anywhere.

"I'll go too," she said.

❧

That night they slept on the deck again, huddling under a piece of canvas to keep the soft, drizzly rain from their faces. The smell of canvas reminded Bridie of the ship from Liverpool. She couldn't sleep. She got out at a lock to walk with the mules for a while.

Crickets hummed and frogs plopped into the

water as the mule team clopped along. The smell of stagnant water and mules filled the air. Silver mist rose from the canal like ghosts.

Bridie walked on one side of the mule team, and Mr. Moody walked on the other. He was acting as hoggee, one of the regular hoggees having gone down with a bout of ague and been left at his aunt's house in Palmyra.

The night air was just a little bit cold on Bridie's face. She put her arm over Sally the mule's back and buried her face for a moment in the warm, mule-smelling flank.

Lantern light from an oncoming barge danced on the water. Bridie heard the hooves of the approaching mule team.

"Upstream barge here," called Mr. Moody. "Give way."

"Ain't gonna give way; we're running light," said the hoggee from the other barge.

"But we're an upstream barge!" said Mr. Moody indignantly.

The other barge drew closer, coming down the canal toward them.

"Get out of our way or we'll chuck you in the ditch," said the stranger. He called out to someone on his boat. "Hey, John, got some trouble here."

A boatman jumped from that barge to the

towpath. He landed on all fours, then got to his feet and looked down at Bridie. "Say, don't I know you?"

His breath reeked of whiskey.

Bridie recognized the voice. She felt as if her stomach had turned to ice. The cold crept all through her, and no amount of fuzzy mule fur could take it away.

"No," she said. Her voice shook, and it was hard to go on.

She looked up through the darkness at a face she hadn't seen in months. Not since it had peered down, dissatisfied, at Bridie's mother's last pay envelope from the woolen mill.

"Ain't you Molly's girl?"

Bridie said nothing. She couldn't. Her throat had closed up. It was not the same as that day at the women's rights convention, when she'd been afraid to speak. Now she was too angry to speak. She hadn't known it was possible to be this angry.

Even when the landlord had come to pull down her family's house in Ireland, she hadn't been this furious. Because then it had seemed like the way things were, with the landlord doing something that had to be done.

But Bridie had changed. Now she knew about human rights.

"You don't know who I am, do you?" said the man, grinning all over his ugly red face.

Behind her in the dark, Mr. Moody and the other hoggee were arguing about which mule team had the right-of-way.

Bridie struggled to find her voice. She thought again about that day at the convention. She had spoken, and people had listened. She could do it again.

"Yes, I know who you are." Her voice shook, so she took a breath and steadied it. "You're John Gerry. You married my mother."

Her teeth were clenched so hard they hurt.

"Heard you two was in the poorhouse," he said. "Get out, did you?"

"She died." Bridie hated even telling him this. He didn't deserve to know.

He stopped grinning. "Well, that's a durn shame. She was a good woman in her way."

Bridie wanted to kick him.

"Still," John Gerry went on, "it's good to know I'm free to find the next Mrs. Gerry."

Bridie wanted to kick him and throw him in the canal.

"Got a sweet little thing in mind already, out in Buffalo," said Mr. Gerry, winking at Bridie. "Good thing I ran into you. And now you, where are you headed, dear?"

"None of your business," said Bridie.

"Suit yourself." John Gerry gave a shrug, and

turned to the hoggee, who was still arguing with Mr. Moody. "Give way, Mike. They're an upstream barge."

Grumbling, the hoggee named Mike unhitched his towrope so that Mr. Moody, Bridie, and the mules could pass.

John Gerry turned to jump back onto his canal boat.

As he bent his knees to leap, Bridie did kick him. Right in the back of one knee. His legs slid from under him and he fell into the canal with an almighty splash.

Mike and Mr. Moody laughed, and the boatmen who were awake on both barges cheered.

Bridie turned away in disgust. Because it *was* like Ireland, it was the way things were. It was like the landlord pulling down the roof, and like Bridie's family wasting away while the wagonloads of grain rolled past on the road. It was the way things *were*.

And the way things were needed to change.

21

CHANGES

The Erie Canal went straight into the heart of Rochester, the great Flour City. The barge glided past mills that sent up a smell of flour and dust as they ground the wheat and other grains of York State.

Bridie and Rose stood on the cabin roof, almost hopping with excitement. Lavinia sat beside them, kicking her legs and looking indifferent.

"I wonder if Mr. Douglass really meant it when he said I could stay with him and go to school," said Rose.

"He wouldn't have said it if he didn't mean it." Bridie was trying to peer down the busy city streets as they slid by. She turned to look up ahead. "People don't say things like that just to—hey! We're going over a bridge?"

Even Lavinia looked slightly interested.

"It's an aqueduct," said Rose knowledgeably. "It carries the canal across the Genesee River."

The mule team walked onto the aqueduct's stone towpath, and the barge floated along behind. The canal was crossing the river. Looking down, Bridie could see the rushing waters of the Genesee chuckling over rocks.

Just the other side of the aqueduct the barge stopped.

"Follow the north star, as they say," said Mr. Moody, pointing. "Go up that street a hundred yards, and you'll see the *North Star* newspaper office right in front of you. You're not the first people we've sent there."

Rose and Bridie thanked him. They said goodbye to the boatmen, the cook, and the mules. Dragging Lavinia, they headed up the street to Frederick Douglass's newspaper.

It was early, and the newspaper office was not open yet.

There was a colored family waiting on the front step—the father leaning in the doorway, the mother beside him, and two little boys sitting on the step at their feet. They looked weary and travel-stained.

The mother nodded a greeting. "Nobody's here yet."

She spoke with a southern drawl that Bridie had trouble understanding.

The man said to Rose, "Have you followed the north star too?"

His accent was as thick as the woman's.

"No, sir, I'm from York State," said Rose.

Just then a white man approached, carrying a key.

"Good morning, all," he said.

The family on the step looked poised to run.

"Have no fears. I'm just Mr. Douglass's printer," the white man said, unlocking the door. "William Nell's the name. He should be along soon. Won't you come in?"

"We'll wait here until he comes, sir," said the father.

You could see in his eyes that he'd seen too much to trust a strange white man, even on the steps of the *North Star*.

The girls followed Mr. Nell into the newspaper office. The place smelled of ink and linseed oil. There were desks with stacks of paper everywhere, and . . . yes, and a big cast-iron printing press in the back.

"Shouldn't we ask their names?" Bridie whispered, glancing back at the family on the steps.

"We don't ask if we don't need to know," Rose whispered back. "They'll probably get new ones soon anyway."

"But should they just be standing there when someone could—"

"This is Rochester," said Rose. "They'll be fine."

Both girls looked at the family. Bridie remembered how she and her mother had walked to Cork to catch the boat to Liverpool, where they'd take ship for America. She thought she almost knew how they felt. Except that the only enemy stalking Bridie and her mother had been hunger.

"Probably fine," Rose added. But she didn't take her eyes off the four people on the doorstep.

Lavinia stood with her arms folded and looked disgusted.

Mr. Nell went over to the press and began fiddling with it. Bridie moved closer to watch, fascinated.

"You girls don't look like the usual morning congregation on the doorstep," Mr. Nell remarked.

"We need to find Mrs. Stanton," said Bridie. "Mrs. Elizabeth Cady Stanton, she's about this tall with curly hair and—"

"Oh, I know Mrs. Stanton well," said Mr. Nell.

"All of the anti-slavery folks know each other; it's a bit depressing when you think about it. Hand me that composing stick."

Bridie handed it to him. "Can you tell us how to find her, please? She's in town for the second-ever women's rights convention."

"She's probably staying with Mrs. Post," said Mr. Nell. "Frederick will know . . . ah, here he comes."

Mr. Douglass ushered the family of fugitives into the office. ". . . two choices, really," he was saying to them. "You can settle in Rochester. York State is free. But the law requires you be turned over to your so-called master if he ever shows up, and Congress is threatening to strengthen that law."

"He'd cross hell barefoot to get us back," said the father.

He didn't say it like he was swearing. Just stating a fact.

"The other choice is Canada," said Mr. Douglass. "We send people on by ship across Lake Ontario, but it takes time to raise the ticket money. Meanwhile, we can squeeze you into the attic at my house. There's a family there already, but they'll be moving on soon."

The man and woman had clearly already decided. "The attic, please," said the woman.

Their children, meanwhile, were staring around

the office. "This is *your* newspaper?" one of them said.

"Say 'sir,'" said his mother.

"Such as it is," said Mr. Douglass.

The two little boys went off to explore.

Mr. Douglass turned to greet the girls. Rose curtsied, and Bridie left the printing press and went over and curtsied too, and Lavinia stood there and stared.

"Young Rose and Phoebe, and . . . is this the missing party?" Mr. Douglass asked, nodding at Lavinia.

"We came on the canal," said Lavinia, still staring.

"Mrs. Stanton sent word back on the train that you were to get on the next one and she'd pay for it," said Mr. Douglass. "She hadn't time to go after you herself. Well, as soon as my messenger boy shows up I'll have him go and fetch her."

Rose and Bridie exchanged a glance. They were to be rid of Lavinia at last.

Bridie went back to watching Mr. Nell set type. She'd been looking at the case and the composing stick before, but not at what the letters were spelling out. Now she looked at the galley, where the newspaper page itself was being assembled.

"That's the Declaration of Sentiments!" she said.

Mr. Nell looked up. "You can read backwards?"

Bridie nodded. "You're printing the whole

thing!" She pointed. "Here's the part about women not being allowed to go to college and have different kinds of jobs."

Jobs like being a printer. Or being a scientist.

"Reading backward is an important knack for a printer," said Mr. Nell. "Can't do the job without it."

Bridie waited for him to say what she hoped he would.

"Would you like to set some type yourself?" he said.

Eagerly, Bridie put on the blue apron he handed her and set to work, picking the letters out of the case. Ƨ-T-H-ᗡ-I-Я . . .

"This girl's got ink in her veins, Frederick," said Mr. Nell.

"Do you need an assistant, Will?" said Mr. Douglass.

Bridie looked at him quickly. She was sure he was joking. But oh, if only he weren't! Imagine getting up every morning and, instead of hauling water and tending the fire and scrubbing and ironing, coming here to set type that would go out into the world forever!

"I could use some extra help," said Mr. Nell, thoughtfully.

Did he really mean it? Bridie couldn't tell. And

Mr. Douglass had gone off to speak to his messenger boy, who had just arrived.

Her heart beating fast, she went back to setting type. Rose drifted over to watch.

"I was just about to write to you, Rose," said Mr. Douglass, coming up. "I've had a letter about your father."

Bridie's hand froze over the letter case. She looked at Rose. Rose looked terrified, and Bridie felt for her. She knew that moment before bad news falls.

Mr. Douglass took a folded paper out of his pocket. "A sailor in New Bedford said he saw your father in England last year."

Bridie wilted with relief, but Rose cried, "Why hasn't he written!"

"Letters go astray," said Mr. Douglass. "I shall be writing to friends in England today to see if they can find out more."

He handed Rose the letter, and she read frantically.

"It will be at least three weeks before I hear back from them," he said. "Probably longer if they need to conduct inquiries."

"Can I stay with you?" Rose blurted. "So that I'll know as soon as you do? Please," she added.

"Certainly. Everyone stays with me. Even William here stays with me." Frederick nodded at the printer. "Mrs. Douglass will be pleased to have another girl around the house—not but that there are quite a few already."

Rose took a deep breath. "And-I-can-go-to-school-with-your-children?" she asked all at once.

"Of course."

Mr. Douglass went back over to the fugitives. Lavinia was wandering around, poking at things. Bridie watched Rose. Rose was still clutching the letter.

"I . . . I'm sure they'll find something out," said Bridie. "Something good, I mean. I hope."

"Someone *saw* him," said Rose.

"If anyone can track him down, Frederick can," said Mr. Nell. "He knows everybody."

There was a commotion at the door, and Mrs. Stanton and Lavinia's mother came in, their wide skirts brushing the door frame. Mrs. Stanton swept past the fugitive family without noticing them, but stopped to talk to Mr. Douglass.

Mrs. Kigley rushed right over and smacked Lavinia on the ear, which Bridie didn't really think was fair under the circumstances. But then, she'd often wanted to smack Lavinia herself.

Mrs. Stanton finished talking to Mr. Douglass and came over to the printing press.

"Good morning, Will." Mrs. Stanton nodded to the printer. "And here you are, girls!" She looked at Bridie, then at Rose, then back at Bridie. "I understand you're the heroines of the hour. How on earth did you get to Rochester?"

"On the Erie Canal," said Rose.

"How very clever and resourceful of you! You simply hopped on a barge?"

"Mr. Moody's barge," said Bridie.

"My landlord," Rose added. "He's a boatman."

"How wonderful. I shall have to try and do something for him."

"I think he would like it better if you didn't," said Rose. "I mean," she added hastily. "Because he was helping, you know, and helping people is what people do and all. . . ." She trailed off.

"No, no, I quite see. You're right, of course, Rose. I hadn't thought."

Bridie looked at Rose and Rose looked at Bridie; it was the first time they could remember Mrs. Stanton saying someone else was right.

"Now," said Mrs. Stanton, "we have to see about getting you girls back to Seneca Falls."

"I'm not going." It was Rose who spoke first, but

Bridie surprised herself by saying the same thing at almost the same time.

"I'm going to stay with the Douglasses." Rose gestured with the letter, now slightly crumpled because she was holding it so tightly. "And go to school. And Mr. Douglass is trying to find my father."

"I see." Mrs. Stanton nodded. "I suppose that makes sense. Well then, Phoebe—"

"I'm not going either," said Bridie.

"Nonsense. You can't stay here. How would you live?"

Bridie took a deep breath. "Mr. Douglass has offered me a job."

She looked toward the door, but Mr. Douglass and the fugitives had left. So had Lavinia and her mother.

She turned to Mr. Nell, waiting to see if he would say that he and Mr. Douglass had been joking, that of course Bridie couldn't be a printer, and that she should go back to Mrs. Stanton's house and dust and scrub and mind children and be glad of it.

"It's true: he did offer her a job, Lizzie," said Mr. Nell.

"But—"

"She's got a natural talent for printing." The printer tapped a section of backward metal print with his knuckle. "There's something in your declaration here about how men have 'monopolized all the profitable employments,' Liz."

"Well, but naturally that refers to being an attorney, or being a physician," said Mrs. Stanton.

"Girl wants to be a printer," said Mr. Nell.

The two adults glared at each other, but half-smiling. They were enjoying the argument, Bridie thought. But it was *her* life. It was time to be heard as well as seen.

"It's true, I do want to be a printer. And I could stay with the Douglasses!" Surely that would be all right. Everyone did, it seemed.

Mrs. Stanton frowned at Bridie, and then at Rose, and then at the still-open door.

She looked at the Declaration of Sentiments, sitting half-finished in the galley.

She seemed to be thinking.

Then she smiled suddenly. "Very well. We shall hate to lose you, but I suppose that *is* what the Declaration means."

Bridie jumped up in the air, she was so happy.

"I'll send your things along, then, when I get back to Seneca Falls," said Mrs. Stanton.

Bridie had things now. She hadn't when she'd first come to the Stantons' a month ago. Now she had a spare apron, and the green hair ribbon Mr. Stanton had given her, and a book Mrs. Stanton had given her called *The American Frugal Housewife*. Besides that, there was a new bonnet she'd bought with her wages. And the wages she hadn't spent, tied up in a red handkerchief.

The stone from her mother's grave, of course, was in her pocket.

"And mine too, please?" said Rose. "We left in kind of a hurry. Mr. Moody will probably bring them for nothing. Oh, and . . . er . . . Tell him I'll pay the rent I owe him when I can."

"One of Frederick's wealthy abolitionist friends has paid it already," said Mrs. Stanton. "So that's no worry."

"Oh." Rose looked somewhat deflated.

"I must be getting back," said Mrs. Stanton. "So goodbye, and good luck, Phoebe and Rose."

Bridie thought about telling Mrs. Stanton that her name wasn't really Phoebe. Then she looked at her friend Rose, who had given her the name. She couldn't hurt Rose's feelings, and Mrs. Stanton didn't need to know.

She could be Bridie and Phoebe both.

"Goodbye, Mrs. Stanton. Tell the boys goodbye for me," said Bridie.

And Rose said goodbye, and Mrs. Stanton left, off to the second-ever women's rights convention.

"You can find out who paid your rent, and pay them back later," Bridie said.

"Or you could not." Mr. Nell found an apron for Rose so she could set type while they waited for Mr. Douglass to come back. "It does people good to give, you know."

Rose put the apron on. "I will, though."

Bridie and Rose hunted out letters. They set out all the words in the Declaration of Sentiments, and they slid them into composing sticks, and set them into the galley.

These words they were setting into print now would go out into the world, starting from a little newspaper office in Rochester—no, starting, really, from Seneca Falls . . . and they would keep going, and Bridie couldn't imagine where they would end up. But she didn't have to.

She was going to be a printer. And she wasn't all alone anymore, she was going to stay with her friend Rose. If the Douglasses didn't mind. And Rose's father might be found. And maybe Rose would grow up to be a scientist even though girls couldn't, and maybe Bridie would grow up to be a printer even though girls didn't.

And maybe someday they'd go to Chicago, that brave new city in the west, or to California, where there were bears and earthquakes and gold. But for now, they were here, and there was work to be done.

HISTORICAL NOTES

The year 1848 was a chaotic one. Revolutions were breaking out all over Europe. Refugees were fleeing famine-stricken Ireland. Gold had just been discovered in California. A deadly cholera pandemic was sweeping the world. In London, Karl Marx wrote *The Communist Manifesto*. In Washington, DC, a treaty was ratified in which Mexico ceded a large portion of its land to the United States.

And in a little town in upstate New York, some women gathered at a tea party and planned the world's first women's rights convention.

The Seneca Falls Convention

The convention was held on July 19 and 20, 1848, and resulted in the adoption of the Declaration of Sentiments. The battle to win the right to vote would last for the next seventy-two years.

If you drew a timeline between the signing of the Declaration of Independence on July 4, 1776,

WOMAN'S RIGHTS CONVENTION.

A Convention to discuss the social, civil, and religious condition and rights of woman will be held in the Wesleyan Chapel, at Seneca Falls, N. Y., on Wednesday and Thursday, the 19th and 20th of July current; commencing at 10 o'clock A. M. During the first day the meeting will be exclusively for women, who are earnestly invited to attend. The public generally are invited to be present on the second day, when Lucretia Mott, of Philadelphia, and other ladies and gentlemen, will address the Convention.*

This ad ran in the *Seneca County Courier* on July 11, 1848.

and the ratification of the Nineteenth Amendment, which gave women the right to vote, on August 18, 1920, the Seneca Falls Convention would fall in the middle . . . almost to the day.

We don't know how many people stayed at the Stanton house during the convention. We know Harriet Cady Eaton and her son, Daniel, did. Lucretia Mott wrote a letter to say she and her husband would be staying, and we know Frederick Douglass had stayed with Stanton on an earlier visit. Since Amy Post traveled with him, it's likely she stayed too. Neither women nor African Americans could count on being welcome at hotels at the time.

Which Characters Are Fictional?

Bridie and Rose are fictional.

Everyone else who attended the women's rights convention and the tea party in Waterloo is real, including the children.

Rose's landlord, Ferris Moody, is real, but the other boatmen are made up.

Most of the other people in Seneca Falls are real.

Rose's teacher is made up. The Kigleys are made up. Elizabeth Cady Stanton and her family are real.

Elizabeth Cady Stanton and two sons in 1848

Stanton ended up having seven children, but only three had been born by 1848.

The people at the poorhouse are made up, but the poorhouse was real.

Frederick Douglass is real, and so is his printer. The family on the doorstep is made up, although many people freeing themselves from slavery did show up on the steps of the *North Star.* Frederick and Anna Douglass sheltered hundreds of fugitives in their house and helped them get to Canada.

The Douglasses always had lots of guests, some of whom stayed for years. So it's perfectly conceiv-

Frederick Douglass

able they would have added Rose and Bridie. At one time the abolitionist John Brown stayed with them. Unlike everyone else, Brown insisted on paying for his room and board.

The Poorhouse

Poorhouses existed in almost every county in the United States. Living conditions ranged from adequate to dismal.

At the time it was opened in 1830, the Seneca County Poorhouse was judged to be adequate by the men who opened it. In 1851, a state commission declared the building uninhabitable. A new poorhouse was built of stone, and still stands. It has been converted into an apartment building, looking very incongruous among the rolling fields and woodlands.

Poorhouses in New York were required to have school for three months a year. In Bridie's day, there was a separate oven house for baking bread, with a schoolroom upstairs. This warm location suggests that the school probably "kept" in the coldest winter months, when there was little work to be done in the fields.

In the twentieth century, social security and other

government programs began to help people in need. The poorhouses had all closed down by the 1970s.

There was probably a poorhouse not far from where you live. It may still be standing but used for something else.

Could Rose's and Bridie's Dreams Really Have Come True?

Could Bridie become a printer? Yes. Even though nearly all skilled trades were closed to women, throughout American history we find exceptions—a female blacksmith here, a female printer there. Often there's no explanation of how they got there. But it must have taken a lot of determination.

Could Rose become a scientist? Again, yes. All colleges except Oberlin were closed to women—but soon that would change. Colleges were only just beginning to teach science, anyway. Science was something one did largely on one's own.

Four woman scientists are mentioned in this book. They are:

Maria Mitchell, an astronomer who discovered a comet in 1847 and later became a professor at Vassar College

Elizabeth Blackwell, who in 1849 became the first woman to graduate from medical school in the United States

Rebecca Lee Davis Crumpler (the "young colored lady" mentioned by Frederick Douglass), who in 1863 became the first African American woman to graduate from medical school in the United States

Eunice Newton Foote, whom Rose and Bridie see by the lemonade stand, who in the 1850s discovered that changing the amount of carbon dioxide in the atmosphere would change the temperature of the earth—the beginning of understanding human-caused climate change

School

The focus of most children's lives was work, not school. Some states had free schools by 1848. New York was one. But you weren't required to go, and in most communities the school only "kept" for two or three months in the winter, and sometimes two or three months in the summer.

Children learned reading, spelling, and handwriting. They moved on to more advanced subjects if they stayed long enough, including a little math. Girls were only taught to add, subtract, multiply, and divide whole numbers.

The textbooks Rose has are all real. Her *New York Reader No. 3* wasn't a third-grade book; schools weren't organized into grades. The anti-slavery dialogue she is made to read is real. The textbook was first published while New York was still a slave state.

In 1855 the textbook Rose quotes from was changed to say that girls *should* have the same education as boys. Change was coming, slowly.

There was usually only one math book, and it went all the way from very simple problems to very complex ones. You bought your own books. Schoolbooks cost eight cents each, a real bargain. Most other books cost twenty-five cents.

Were the schools segregated? In New York State in 1848, it depended on the school, the school board, and the teacher.

In Rochester, Frederick Douglass had continual fights to keep his children in school. Sometimes he hired a governess to teach them at home.

Elizabeth Cady Stanton and Abolitionism

In 1848 there were about 2.5 million people enslaved in the United States—and the number was increasing. The addition of vast new territories acquired from Mexico meant that slavery could increase even more. That was the battle that Elizabeth Cady Stanton's husband, Henry, was fighting in the summer of 1848.

Elizabeth Cady was born in 1815 to a wealthy upstate New York family that enslaved at least three people. As a teenager she was converted to anti-slavery by her much-older cousin, Gerrit Smith. He also introduced her to the abolitionist Henry Stanton, whom she married against her parents' wishes.

Elizabeth Cady Stanton's commitment was to women's rights, not abolitionism. When it comes to anti-slavery, we see her agreeing with the people around her—nearly everyone she spent time with was an abolitionist—but not taking action on her own.

After the Civil War, the Fourteenth and Fifteenth Amendments gave African American men the right to vote. Elizabeth Cady Stanton and her friend Susan B. Anthony strongly opposed the amendments because women had not been included. This caused a split between them and the other human rights activists, including Frederick Douglass. In her speeches in these later years, Stanton sometimes used insulting language to describe African Americans.

The Irish Potato Famine

The Irish potato famine lasted from 1845 to 1849. It was caused by a mold called *Phytophthora infestans,* which flourishes in cool, wet weather. Today it is better known as "late blight." It still devastates tomato and potato crops.

It was disastrous in Ireland because many people lived entirely on potatoes and had no access to any other food, and because the blight recurred for several years. The British government, which ruled Ireland at the time, did not do enough to help the starving Irish.

English landlords owned big Irish estates where families like Bridie's lived. The landlords exported the grain grown on their estates to England while their Irish tenants starved. When the tenants couldn't pay their rent, the landlords pulled down the cottages. The landlords wanted to have fewer tenants; in fact, they wanted there to be fewer Irish people. Some landlords paid for ships to take their tenants to the New World. Some of the ships were in bad shape, and so were the tenants. These unseaworthy hulks were the so-called "coffin ships." Many of the refugees did not arrive alive.

The population of Ireland has never returned to pre-famine numbers. The ruins of the pulled-down stone cottages can still be seen in the Irish countryside today.

This picture from *The Illustrated London News* in 1848 shows an Irish family's house being torn down.

Phrenology

Phrenology was the study of natural bumps on the head. It was thought that from the shape of a person's skull you could learn about his or her personality traits, abilities, and intelligence. Feeling someone's bumps and consulting a phrenology chart could tell you all about them.

A phrenology diagram from 1834

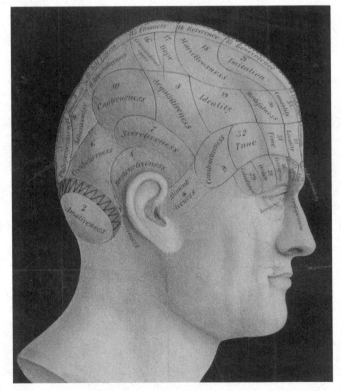

It was nonsense, of course. Different parts of the brain do govern different abilities, but you can't tell how someone's brain works by looking at or feeling their skull. The skull is bone, not brain.

Many intelligent people—including Stanton—believed in phrenology. But these people also liked to tell stories about how someone's personality turned out to be *completely different* from what the bumps said it should be.

Changes in Scenery in New York State Since 1848

The state is no longer referred to as "York State," as it often was in the nineteenth century.

Wheat is no longer a major crop in New York State, but it was in 1848.

The Erie Canal no longer goes into downtown Rochester. It was rerouted in the twentieth century, and today passes through the outskirts of the city.

The longest bridge in the Western Hemisphere is long gone. Instead of crossing Cayuga Lake, travelers today drive through the Montezuma Swamp on US Route 20. (Look for eagle nests.)

The Flats, the islands in the Seneca River where many factories stood, are now underneath Van

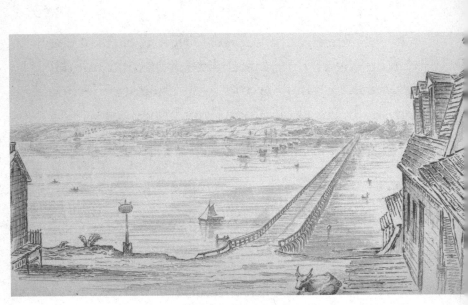

Cayuga Long Bridge

Cleef Lake. There are no waterfalls in Seneca Falls now; they are also under the lake.

Malaria is no longer endemic to Seneca Falls.

The modern locks on the Cayuga & Seneca Canal are not in the same places as the locks of 1848.

Elizabeth Cady Stanton's house still stands, but is smaller than it was. The Wesleyan Chapel, where the convention was held, is a replica. These sites are operated by the National Park Service and can be visited in the summer months.

There is much more wildlife in New York State than there was in 1848. Species that were driven to near extinction in the northeastern United States in the eighteenth and nineteenth centuries have since been reintroduced or have recovered on their own. Rose and Bridie do not see deer, small mammals, wild turkeys, eagles, or great blue herons. But if you follow the route they took, you might.

ACKNOWLEDGMENTS

I am very grateful to the staff at the Women's Rights National Historical Park in Seneca Falls, New York. Education specialist Denise DeLucia and rangers Rebecca Weaver and Kyle Harvey provided me with all kinds of historical details large and small. Visual information specialist Zack/Cora Frank went out to take some video to answer one of my questions, in the middle of a polar vortex when the temperature was -10°F. You are all wonderful!

Many thanks also to:

Ranger Rita Knox at the Chesapeake and Ohio Canal National Historical Park (which actually has real live mule-drawn boats) for explaining the intricacies of mule team right-of-way and how mule teams pass through locks;

Lori D. Ginzberg, author of *Elizabeth Cady Stanton: An American Life*, for answering my questions and providing insights into Stanton's character;

Gregory Hays for helping me research the

grammatical rules of Quaker *thee* and *thy*, which are very different from the rules for the archaic English pronouns *thou*, *thee*, and *thy*;

Marsha Watson, Joyce Witkowski, and other staff at the Fred & Harriet Taylor Memorial Library, who tracked down many obscure books for me, including one about New York State railroads in the 1840s;

Tammy L. Brown, associate professor at Miami University, who checked the manuscript for historical accuracy;

and Aaron Schwabach, who helped me track down weird old laws and words.

And thanks to Diane Landolf, Caitlin Blasdell, and Joel Naftali for everything.

Any errors that remain are my own.